BARSA KELMES

BARSA KELMES

THE NOMADS RETURN

GABIT BEKAKHMETOV

NEW DEGREE PRESS

BARSA KELMES

The Nomads Return

ISBN   979-8-88504-554-4   *Paperback*

979-8-88504-880-4   *Kindle Ebook*

979-8-88504-671-8   *Ebook*

for the children of the steppe

CONTENTS

The plot is laid: if all things fall out right,
I shall as famous be by this exploit
As Scythian Tomyris by Cyrus' death.

—SHAKESPEARE, HENRY VI

Man was made a rebel; can rebels be happy? You were
warned... You had no lack of warnings and indications,
but you did not heed the warnings. You rejected the
only way of arranging for human happiness, but for-
tunately, on your departure, you handed the work over
to us. You promised, you established with your word,
you gave us the right to bind and loose, and surely you
cannot even think of taking this right away from us
now. Why, then, have you come to interfere with us?

—FYODOR DOSTOEVSKY,

THE BROTHERS KARAMAZOV

The Governor of Genoa complained to Mazzini's father
saying that Mazzini was a young man of talent, very
fond of solitary walks at night, and habitually silent as
to the subject of his meditations, and that the Govern-
ment was not fond of young men of talent, the subject
of whose musings was unknown to it.

—C. EDMUND MAURICE,

THE REVOLUTIONARY MOVEMENT OF 1848-9

AUTHOR'S NOTE

When I think of my childhood, the first image that comes to mind is the blue sky. I used to spend every summer from ages three to nine at a nomadic camp in Kazakhstan. Growing up with sheep, marmots, steppe foxes, horses, and eagles made nature a big part of my life. A yurt or an old train wagon was all I needed to sleep in. The rest of the time I spent on the steppe, watching the sky and singing songs. Even though this all happened in the Soviet Union in the 1980s, some traces of the nomadic past were still left. Recently, while visiting an outdoor museum in Turkestan, I noticed a nineteenth-century wheel very similar to the ones we used in the camp. It is very difficult to find an authentic nomadic setting nowadays, but the world is shifting back to nomadic values. People are almost as obsessed with sustainability as the nomads were. I remember how my grandparents would see to it that we, as a camp, produced no waste. Everything was utilized either by animals or by people. Fortunately, we didn't have any plastic bottles back then.

Eurasian nomads used to be a force to be reckoned with. Their ways of life and values produced some of the most notorious leaders in world history, such as Attila the Hun,

Genghis Khan, and Tamerlane. Conquering the world was a by-product of constant innovations in the steppe. Domestication of the horse, according to historians, happened in the north of Kazakhstan. So did the invention of the chariot, the development of nomadic bows, and the crafting of world-class military strategies. Nomads spent a lot of time along the Silk Road facilitating global trade, spreading ideas, and scaling innovations. It is a shame that our current nation-state ideologies prevent nomads from enjoying their traditional routes. They must now confine themselves to limited territories—often with no access to water and grasslands, thanks to global warming.

As the world is now frantic with innovation, globalization, and interplanetary travel spearheaded by Silicon Valley moguls and universe-conquerors, nomadic ideas are becoming relevant once again. Do we really need to be sedentary? Do we even need to stick to Earth? Looking at the blue sky, we realize the universe is infinite, and we want to explore it. Perhaps, we can revive nomadic ideals once again, even if we fail to revive the nomadism that we so cruelly destroyed. I wrote this work of fiction to explore this idea, bringing the last rulers of Christian, Buddhist, and Muslim nomads back to life. I hope you will find them to be intriguing characters.

Writing a work of fiction in a borrowed language is an ambitious endeavor. Some stories, however, cannot be told in any other way. This is especially true when a story explores post-colonial landscapes and when the languages at the author's disposal are imbibed with a corresponding ethos. In such situations, it is actually easier to employ a third language. Unsurprisingly, English is that other language, as it represents the business, politics, and the culture of the West in Central Asian affairs. Aggressively learned and imported by the locals, English, for the former nomads, represents a chance not only to catch up with but also to surpass the Russians and the Chinese.

If you are interested in the affairs of Central Asia, you will inherently understand it is impossible to discuss the area without also knowing the culture and history of the great empires surrounding the nomads. I highly recommend visiting our part of the world and recreating the travels of Marco Polo. In the meantime, let this story transport you into the region and its history.

PROLOGUE

——

1750, Burabay, Middle Horde, Qazaq Khanate
Topysh the Beautiful felt extremely satisfied with the day's yoga practice. Jumbaktas the Mystery Stone, peeping out of the mirror-like lake, was one of the best places for meditation. The Tibetan master, brought to Burabay specifically for her, was a true guru. She had not met such a source of wisdom and harmony since her childhood days at her father's court, where she was surrounded by students of the great Zaya Pandita.

If only those Kazakhs could learn to relax more and stop making life stressful for each other... Topysh thought, even as the hope behind these words was obscured by clouds. Scheming and strategizing seemed to preoccupy most of even her beloved husband Abylai Khan's time. And now, entering their yurt, she could sense the Khan's mind was not in the present at the moment. He was worried and anxious about something. As always.

"Where are your thoughts flying, my Khan?"

"Oh, *janym*, my soul, I am still thinking about that strange dream from last night..."

"What makes you think it was anything more than a dream? Try not to worry about it. Maybe it was what the Russians call *koshmar*, just another scary vision?"

"It was not a *koshmar*. And it is not Russian but French. Sorry. I have seen scarier things in life. This was a warning, but it appears to be beyond my control; it is beyond my time and yours."

"What did you see? Perhaps I can interpret it favorably." She found dream interpretation to be an enjoyable pastime in the steppe. It also made her feel more powerful than other wives of the Khan.

"I saw a Kashgari merchant sitting alone in his atlas robe under the Lonely Tree, telling me of his own dream. He described a three-headed dragon that inhabited the backbone of the Earth. The left head had curly yellow hair and big blue eyes. The right head had straight black hair and small dark eyes. The middle head was like that strange animal of which Sultan Baybars used to write to Berke Khan. It could change its color according to its environment. It was a magnificent dragon, a beauty to behold. It was noble and strong. What scared the Kashgari was that right before the end of the Time as we know it, the dragon started losing each of its heads one by one. First it lost its left head, then it lost its right head, and then it lost its middle head."

Understanding her husband's dream as a terrible warning, Topysh the Beautiful started crying. Her decision not to interpret the dream prompted the Khan to sacrifice a white camel.

PART I

KENESARY THE CLONE

CHAPTER 1

NOSTALGIA

———

2021, Almaty, Kazakhstan

During a particularly unusual day, Professor Ansar Tolengitovich, Director of the Institute of Molecular Biology, felt like the world as he knew it was about to end. This strange feeling came to him as he walked along the same Al-Farabi University Road that had borne his deliberate and measured footsteps for the last forty years. Stretched along the Botanical Garden, the street was one of the few places left in the city with satisfactory levels of oxygen.

Back straight and eyes aloft, he noticed once again how the students relying on the same road had changed completely from those of his distant memories. Less reliant than dependent, even the young people who had recently come from villages strolled along more like city dwellers. The young men particularly weren't as masculine and brutal anymore, neither in gait nor expression, not even like he and his friends had been in Soviet times. Forget resembling their glorious nomad ancestors, who could boast of being able to conquer any city, country, or empire.

When his cousin's grandson passed by and failed to greet him, the professor became even more nostalgic. He remembered his native village near Baikonur, where they used to gather to watch rockets fly into space, yet the boys would never cut across their elders' paths, not even in an enthusiastic rush. Somehow, modern scientific achievements and millennia-old traditions did not seem to conflict with each other back then. Yes, now that he thought about it, he was lucky. He had gotten a sense of the best of both worlds: traces of the nomadic past and echoes of the technological future, all while building communism on Earth. Those times appeared to be good in retrospect.

Then again, memory is a professional trickster. He remembered his veteran uncles who would nostalgically recount tales of glory from World War II, longing for an opportunity to go back to those times, perhaps to visit Western Europe once again. Six hundred thousand brave young Kazakhs went to Europe in that bloody war, a lot more than even the Golden Horde could gather at its peak. This brought the professor back to his lamentations. The current generation, he judged with his hands tightening behind his back, was not as courageous or patriotic as the heroes near or far, too heavily influenced by the strange Russians and even stranger Americans to be found on all kinds of social media.

The professor remembered his grandfather, Saduaqas, who was born in the 1880s and witnessed many uprisings, revolutions, famines, collectivization efforts, labor camps, purges, and world wars. *Why is he always silent?* the professor used to wonder as a child, looking at his grandfather. Saduaqas never talked about his ancestors, nor his religion. He secretly performed *namaz* in a small prayer room and rarely mentioned *Allah* in the presence of his grandchildren.

He much preferred to talk about Lenin, inserting him as the protagonist when he read them short stories from *One Thousand and One Nights*. In these stories, however, Lenin the Shoemaker or Lenin the Sailor would always end up marrying the shah's daughter or becoming chief vizier to the khalif but never killing them or their families. Secretly, Saduaqas must have wished that Lenin were indeed only a character from fiction. After all, Lenin's follower, evil Goloshchekin, had destroyed all of Saduaqas's brothers and uncles. What good could one expect from the man who killed the Russian emperor and all his family?

Still, the later part of Soviet history had certainly been good, mainly because the professor had been young and healthy. His parents were alive, his friends were around, and there was some sort of expectation… *the wind of change.* That special "atmosphere" was filled with so much positive energy and warmth. Even the dangerous 1990s were not too bad in retrospect. Yes, millions of people left Kazakhstan for Germany, Israel, the USA, and Russia. But millions more stayed, believed in the president, and waited for the "Kazakhstan 2030" vision to materialize. Indeed, the professor could still remember a large poster with a snow leopard jumping toward a brightly typed "2030" on this very street. The snow leopard, of course, represented Kazakhstan. It was supposed to be faster than the "Asian tigers."

Those images from the past belonged to some other dimension now, and the professor had a very difficult time adjusting to the new reality. Especially after the Great Pandemic, things had changed dramatically. Walk and talk-loving "Almatians," which is what the dog-loving professor called the fine people of Almaty, were now completely domesticated. Like cats, they would sit in their apartments, watching their screens and rarely going out. Neighbors hardly knew each other. Other people's children, even those of close relatives, would not recognize their old Ansar *ata* on his rare visits.

One positive outcome, for the professor at any rate, was that based on millions of PCR tests for a coronavirus, intentionally nebulous authorities were able to collect every person's DNA in Kazakhstan. This amazing collection of data intrigued Ansar Tolengitovich, not only because of its applications in genomics and molecular biology but also because of its importance for history and genealogy, the professor's other favorite topics. Never in his life could he have dreamt that in a matter of only a couple of years, he would be gifted the whole country's gene pool.

The professor, turning the last corner, knew who was in fact related to whom. He knew it better than the people themselves. It was dangerous knowledge, which is why he had to sign a Non-Disclosure Agreement with the Committee of National Security, also known as the KNB, Kazakhstan's successor to the KGB. The professor liked these KNB people; they were cool, not as bad as KGB guys were. But then again, maybe KNB officers did not have much work to do and did not feel any pressing need to be too bad because everyone was supplying the information the KNB needed through their smart phones anyway.

Stop thinking about KNB and KGB. Their job is not an easy one, thought the professor, as he reached his apartment. His friends, who would occasionally visit him in the lab, still turned off their phones and put them under their bottoms so that the borderline-magical devices would not transmit whatever secrets or overly liberal ideas they entertained. "Stop flattering yourselves," the professor would joke, but he would find himself equally paranoid and doing the same thing, especially when discussing politics. After three turns of an old key, the professor's huge alabai, Ayu, greeted him with so much joy that thanks to the Kazakh shepherd dog the professor's nostalgia all but disappeared.

The next morning, out of old habit, Ansar Tolengitovich turned on his TV. He had stopped paying for cable since YouTube and Netflix provided all the content he needed. Much like in the Soviet Union, he enjoyed having only two stations. It was no longer necessary to juggle among hundreds of strange channels. Over the sound of water boiling for tea, the anchor lady on YouTube news talked about the president's attempts to retrieve the head of the last Khan of the Kazakhs, Kenesary, who was betrayed by his allies before being deceived and beheaded by a tribal leader in Kyrgyzstan in the nineteenth century. The head had been delivered to some Russian official in Western Siberia. Since then, Kazakhs had been trying to repatriate Kenesary's head for almost two centuries to offer the Khan a proper funeral. The whole affair sounded completely ridiculous to the professor.

"What would you do with the head? It's not even a head anymore; it's probably just a skull," said the professor, looking for validation from his only companion at home. Ayu cocked his head, seeming to consider the question to be an important one.

"Russians return the dead only when they start losing a war," the professor went on, continuing his morning conversation with the curious Ayu. He was referring to Stalin's order to return the world conqueror Tamerlane's corpse back to its resting place in Samarkand in the darkest days of World War II. Lo and behold, the tide of events on the Western front changed significantly as Tamerlane found his comfort at the feet of Sultan Baraka, his teacher and spiritual master. The professor again felt nostalgic as he remembered his child-hood trip to Moscow to visit Lenin's Mausoleum, where poor Vladimir Ulyanov's corpse was still kept intact. *Why is Russia so obsessed with the dead?* wondered the professor.

As he thought more about it, a random idea crossed his mind: *What if Lenin is in some sort of advanced hiberna-tion mode?*

This sounded outrageous, but under certain circum-stances not entirely impossible. He shrugged it off, but his next idea was even bolder: *If the Russians do not return Kene-sary's head, we should clone Kenesary.* Dismissed, dismissed! Or, well... perhaps this was actually possible, especially in light of recent archeological findings near Issyk-Kul, which had finally gotten rid of interfering tourists during the Great Pandemic.

Ansar Tolengitovich had an archeologist friend from their student years who had told him secretly that they found a likely burial place of the Khan and his warriors. Surely, this friend could take him to the burial site if they went for a weekend to Kyrgyzstan. If he succeeded in obtaining some small sample of a Khan candidate's DNA, he could easily match it to Y chromosomes of Genghis Khan's descendants and confirm if the body did indeed belong to the de-height-ened Kenesary. After all, Kazakhstan was home to thousands of those royal descendants who called themselves *töre*. Their DNA samples, of course, were kept in a special refrigerator.

Work passed by slower than usual and, on his walk back home, Ansar Tolengitovich felt a strong urge to smoke a cig-arette. Unfortunately, his coronavirus-survivor lungs were no longer any good, and he did not want to put them at risk. His thoughts once again turned to poor Kenesary. Oh, what an achievement it would be to bring him back! Forget about his skull. The whole man could come back in the twenty-first century.

It would even be possible to edit his genome a little bit with some CRISPR technology to make him more resistant to coronavirus, HIV and all kinds of other parasites that make city life more difficult. Of course, if one Chinese professor had managed to edit the genes of the twin girls born in that strict Communist country, it would be easy to cover up gene editing in a relaxed liberal state like Kazakhstan. But then it would not really be Kenesary. It was important for the Khan to return as he had been, in his true genetic manifestation. That way Kazakhs would not question that he was a pure *töre*, ready to reclaim his throne and bring back the nomadic civilization destroyed by Lenin, Stalin, Goloshchekin, and the like. Ansar Tolengitovich's hands gripped each other behind his back with something like excitement. Perhaps, if this were to happen, these fragile men on campus would end up a little bit more polite and manly.

CHAPTER 2

THE GOLDEN MAN

—

2021, Almaty, Kazakhstan

About ten kilometers north of, or rather, as the more fortunate residents of the upper Almaty liked to point out, around five hundred meters *below* the university campus, lived Mels Abdulhamidovich in a district called Mirror Springs near the world famous *baraholka* market. He had assured the truth of that latter distinction himself, when in 1993 he took an American friend to that market to purchase a rug. He considered himself a rather good friend in that regard, certainly one that Ansar Tolengitovich should be grateful for.

It was very tempting to address Mels Abdulhamidovich as Professor because all his neighbors referred to him in such a manner. Despite their old friendship, however, such a thing would be a step too far for the esteemed Director of the Institute of Molecular Biology. In truth, Mels had never really completed his doctorate. If cornered on the issue, he would, of course, claim that a doctorate was overrated and that many of those scientists with PhDs knew absolutely everything about close to nothing.

Deep down, however, he regretted not having completed his doctorate in the early 1990s. Instead of focusing on writing his dissertation, he had decided to look for gold along with some other adventurous archeologists. They were sure that the Steppe, finally free from the Soviets, favored the risk-takers, and they would find yet another Golden Man with just a bit of ethical tomb raiding.

Mels was so named after Marx, Engels, Lenin, and Stalin by a talented teacher, Abdulhamid, who had high hopes for his first child. Abdulhamid himself had never gotten any of the numerous Soviet state recognitions or rewards for his otherwise impeccable teaching record, thanks to his somewhat Islamic name. His fast-growing beard, extremely unusual for men of the Northern parts of Kazakhstan, also did not help with the progression of his career. Nevertheless, Abdulhamid was highly regarded by his colleagues and the community.

Most importantly, his students always remembered him, sending him greeting cards from the prestigious universities of Leningrad, Moscow, Tashkent, and Almaty. Lacking any diplomas or awards to hang on the walls of his little study room, Abdulhamid took particular pride in showcasing those greeting cards. Little Mels grew up among those cards, learning the names of different statues, architectural buildings, and beautiful nature sites that so often ended up being featured on envelopes, cards, stamps and other products of the conservative Soviet postal system, which was heir to the *yam* system invented by Genghis Khan himself.

It was only natural, therefore, that after high school, Mels decided to go to Almaty, then capital of the Kazakh Soviet Socialist Republic and simply a beautiful city. Back then Al-Farabi Kazakh National University was named after Kirov, a Soviet revolutionary and a close friend of Stalin. There Mels met Ansar Tolengitovich, who was studying biology. The university dorm housed students from different departments together, so the campus environment was full of ideas and discussions.

Majoring in archeology, Mels did indeed benefit greatly from Ansar's impressive books on zoology, botany, human anatomy, ecology, evolution, and, of course, genetics. Even though the whole world had its eyes eagerly trained on new advancements and innovations in that last field, the Soviet Union of the 1980s had a rather short history of achievements to its credit, mostly because of Trofim Lysenko, the notorious Director of the Institute of Genetics.

Lysenko was responsible for defaming and murdering thousands of Soviet biologists before World War II. Since the end of Lysenkoism, however, a lot of new energy was put into genetic research and Ansar Tolengitovich was among the talented students who were recruited through the all-Soviet Biology Olympiad. The Party saw the cell as the next cosmos with a lot to discover.

In archeology, on the other hand, the glory days seemed to have already passed. Professor Akishev had already discovered the famous Golden Man, a Saka warrior in golden armor from the sixth century BC. He had also already discovered the remains of the legendary city of Otrar in the south of Kazakhstan, where philosopher and mathematician Al-Farabi (called "the Second Teacher after Aristotle" by Saint Thomas Aquinas) was born.

Dismayed, Mels felt the only discovery that would make him famous would be finding Genghis Khan's grave. After *perestroika*, however, our professor-to-never-be figured it would be more realistic to look for another Golden Man. To find him, he thought, he would need to expand his search area, because it would be very difficult to compete with Professor Akishev in his natural habitat. Kyrgyzstan, therefore, was an obvious choice.

Arriving in Bishkek in the early 1990s, Mels encountered a city that had certainly seen better times. With so many people leaving the Kyrgyz capital, Mels found himself in an environment that was transitioning into poverty. With it came crime. Drug trafficking, in particular, made it difficult for Mels to feel safe in the mountains, even with his loyal archeologist adventurers. Instead of Golden Men, they more often stumbled upon recent corpses.

Nevertheless, Mels got to know the Kyrgyz culture pretty well, picked up local language skills, and made some lasting acquaintances at the impoverished Bishkek Archeology Institute, ironically abbreviated BAI, which means *rich*. Yet as their mission grew more dangerous, Mels figured it would be safer to return to Almaty.

At home Mels spent his time working at a local city library, and somehow, among the books, thirty years flew by.

It was, therefore, slightly unexpected but quite pleasing to receive a call from Ansar Tolengitovich. Working in a library near the *baraholka bazaar* is tantamount to operating a tobacco shop in a tuberculosis sanatorium. Bazaar people have little attention span left for books, especially for those decrepit Soviet books still constituting the majority of Mels Abdulhamidovich's collection. As much as Mels hoped to chat to his old friend, Ansar cut the conversation short and invited the curious bookkeeper to visit him in the evening.

Once there, the first thing to greet Mels was an enormous canine. *It is great to see Ansar's Ayu again. What a huge alabai dog!* Mels had seen such dogs' skeletons during the excavations at Botai settlements in the north of Kazakhstan.

"It is actually strange that such a conservative Kazakh man as you would keep a dog in an apartment," said Mels.

The professor chuckled.

"I never thought I would do such a Russian thing myself, but you know how difficult it was last year. I could not stand sitting alone in this bubble yurt in the air. I hate apartments!"

Ansar's thoughts were always on the pandemic. He had lost too many relatives and friends to the calamity. In the very first month, even before the lockdowns, the professor had lost his dear wife, who already had a pre-existing condition. He wished they'd had children together, but it did not work out when they were young, and they simply never discussed the matter again.

"You are a solitary wolf, my friend. But sometimes even our loneliness needs to be shared. I am glad you did not get a Dachshund…" Mels trailed off a bit before adding, "An alabai is a good friend for a wolf like you."

The teapot started boiling and the friends sat to drink. Foregoing small talk, Ansar quickly began sharing his idea and even wore his eyeglasses to show that he was absolutely intent on going to the recently discovered graveyard in Kyrgyzstan to find Kenesary's body, with or without Mels.

Sipping his tea with much seriousness and enjoyment, savoring the moment, Mels cut in, "We will find him, my friend. It will be very easy to identify his body."

"How is that?" asked the professor.

"Because he does not have a head," said Mels, offering a rare but highly promising grin.

On Friday evening, Mels and the professor jumped on a Bishkek-bound minivan that they ordered through the inDriver app. It was a beautiful serpentine trip through the mountains. The adventurers reserved the whole car for themselves so they could make some important calls to their Kyrgyz friends on the way, hopefully making it easier to find Kenesary's body. The location they had set as their ultimate destination matched historical details about the fight that took place between Kenesary and the violent tribal leader who had beheaded him. Both Mels and Ansar were excited about meeting their colleagues in Bishkek.

After talking to the archeologists of the BAI, Mels could feel that Kyrgyzstan in the 2020s was a lot different from Kyrgyzstan in the 1990s. This was a democracy—a poor one but real. After revolutions of all kinds and colors, the country had finally consolidated its political system. This seemed to give Kyrgyz people the right to feel proud of their freedom and act slightly arrogant toward their Kazakh neighbors. At least that was the impression Mels and Ansar got, noticing with some unfamiliar envy how almost no one hid their smartphones under their bottoms when sharing their real feelings about their government.

"If you feel they are being haughty, remind them of their treason. They should not have sold Kenesary's head to the Russians." Ansar Tolengitovich, of course, was half-joking. He perfectly understood that the Kyrgyz had already paid for their crime by sending one hundred of their best sons to the Middle Horde in the nineteenth century. Their descendants still lived among the Kazakhs and had intermarried with the locals, producing many famous poets and heroes. The matter, therefore, was settled a long time ago, and it would be vile and vulgar to keep remembering the episode. *Only people as bored and obsessed with historical grudges as fascists should engage in such useless conversations*, thought Ansar.

The lights went out, but Mels was excited and could not sleep that night. Finally, he was about to do something serious in archeology. Not simply to find a Golden Man but to return one of golden lineage, *altyn urpaq*, to life! It was a great honor, and Mels decided that should the mission succeed, he would do his best to educate and train the young Kenesary. Based on his experience in Kazakhstan, he knew it was important to stay close to influential people. Who could be more potentially powerful than a clone of the last khan of the Kazakhs? Even the presidents had been discussing his skull at important meetings. They would surely see to it that Kenesary's clone was a rich man. This was an opportunity of a lifetime for a *baraholka* librarian.

* * *

The next day, the team arrived in the area around Lake Issyk-Kul, climbed the mountains, and eventually reached the small graveyard with one particularly visible tomb. Mels, experienced in all matters related to graves of important people, suddenly exclaimed: "This is it! This is Kenesary's grave." Ansar took off his eyeglasses, took a deep breath, and said: "On your own head be it if you are wrong!"

Fortunately, the site was located so high in the mountains they could hope for the body to be slightly frozen and well-preserved. They stood around the grave in silence, not expecting to be feeling the weight of committing the sin of exhumation. Everyone wanted to bring back Kenesary, but perhaps that made them see him as already living, a being that could be insulted.

Ansar Tolengitovich picked up the shovel, reassuring himself of the historical importance of the situation.

Pushing out of his mind how upset his grandfather Sad-uaqas would be with this, Ansar kept telling himself he only needed a tiny sample of DNA, nothing else. Finally, two meters below the surface of the earth, his shovel was stopped by a royal shield.

CHAPTER 3

THE VIRTUOUS MOTHER

2021, Kyzylorda, Kazakhstan

From Bishkek, the two friends decided to head back over the border to Taraz and then to Kyzylorda, a Kazakh city nearby whose name translates to *The Red Horde*. As many "reds" had done before them, Ansar and Mels had brought a bottle of Mongolian vodka called *Chinggis Khan* to celebrate their triumph. For these old school Soviet gentlemen, any kind of serious discussion was incomplete without vodka. They indulged in nodding to their own peculiar brand of romantic patriotism with the selection, enjoying that meltwater from a sacred mountain's snow had been used to finish their evening drink. Fresh fish from the local Syr Darya River, better known as Jaxartes and Seyhun, gilded the lily, making this special dinner unforgettable.

Kyzylorda had seen its fair share of triumphant gentlemen in the past, counting as its guests such diverse luminaries as the first cosmonauts who dared to slip the surly bonds of Earth for country and party, the irrigation engineers whose disastrous plans made the description of the city as "nearby the Aral Sea" less true with every passing year, and the Red

Army generals who made Central Asia a place where such doings and more could transpire, regardless of the thoughts of the locals. More recently, Chinese engineers implementing Belt and Road infrastructure projects had arrived in the area, revitalizing old trade routes.

Our two heroes, however, had an even more historical role to play, especially for the local population, ninety-seven percent of which was comprised of Kazakhs. This statistical fact had attracted the professor's attention. For the part of Kenesary's mother, he wanted to choose a pure Kazakh, not only a fluent speaker of the language but a genuine practitioner of the nationality. Such a person could not be found in Almaty or Shymkent, which were under some Russian and Uzbek cultural influences. So, at least, thought Ansar, as he poured another glass of vodka for himself and Mels.

Our adventurers came to Kyzylorda for one more reason— Barsa-Kelmes, a former island that was home to a nature reserve where many near-extinct species, such as the Pleistocene *Saiga tatarica* and the wild Kulan horse, were able to flourish. A secret biological laboratory on the island had been, in its better days, one of the top bioweapon facilities of the Soviet Union. It was rumored that the world-famous anthrax, for example, was developed in *The Red Horde*'s very own Barsa-Kelmes. This former island, united against its will with its powerful neighbors, was an ideal place to give birth to and educate the last khan of the Kazakhs, who would restore a nomadic style of living. But how to find a virtuous mother for Kenesary? As the evening wore on, and not unexpectedly, the afterthought that was the woman became the only thought that mattered.

Ansar elucidated his thoughts. He wanted her to be Muslim but not too Muslim; Kazakh, but not fake Kazakh;

neither a city lady nor a village woman; not too young nor too old. He definitely did not want her to belong to the ruling party. Ansar had no information on the historical Kenesary's mother, but ideally, a mother of the khan should belong to the Konyrat tribe because Genghis Khan's mother and wife were Konyrats. As the list of requirements grew, he started to despair, only to remind himself that all he really needed was to raise a healthy, intelligent boy who could be fit to rule the country. Mels agreed that this should not be such a tall order; he also suggested it would help if Ansar officially married the lady because boys needed to grow up seeing their fathers to learn how to be leaders.

"That's not true," needled Ansar. "Think about Jesus and Muhammad. Did they have fathers when they were growing up?"

"I refuse to comment on Jesus, but Muhammad grew up with his grandfather and numerous uncles. Surely, they played an important role in his upbringing." Mels, who prided his matchmaking skills from behind a librarian's desk, was pressing to use this historic opportunity to get his friend a companion—a human one. "Even Abylai Khan grew up under the strong mentorship of Tole bi. You can't just leave the boy with a random woman in Barsa-Kelmes. It doesn't work that way, my friend."

"That's true. Oh, Allah! Can you imagine all the jokes I will hear, that in my sixties I decided to marry a young lady?"

"You will hear more jokes if you do not marry her, Ansar. Remember all those people named after numbers, such as Fifty, Sixty, Seventy, and Eighty in your childhood? You know why they were given these age-ist names?"

"Haha, yes. Kazakhs in the past were strong, the wonders of a unique keto diet. They could indeed have children when they were sixty, seventy, or even eighty. Now our old men can barely walk."

Mels could feel that Ansar was warming up to the idea. Some of Ansar's more prosperous friends had unofficial second wives, or official lovers, who people called *toqals*. Ansar had never wanted a *toqal* out of respect for his dear wife. Now that he was a widower, however, his new wife would not technically be a *toqal* although she would be significantly younger than him and would probably be thought of as one. Ansar also knew it would be extremely difficult to persuade a Kazakh woman to give birth to a child out of wedlock, a khan though the bastard may be. On the other hand, a marriage to a successful professor with a nice apartment in the Golden Quad of Almaty? That might very well be an entirely different matter.

* * *

Tomyris never liked her name. It sounded tomboyish and not very Kazakh. After Akan Satayev's blockbuster movie *Tomyris* was released, however, her name went viral and became a hot topic of conversation. Suddenly many of her friends with more popular "Ai" (*Moon*) and "Gul" (*Flower*)-based names started showing small signs of envy. She would often be asked lighthearted questions based on the movie, such as "Would you behead someone like Cyrus as well if he killed your boyfriend?" Unfortunately, Tomyris did not have a boyfriend, maybe (as she told herself) because she was always busy either working at the hotel or studying philosophy. Nevertheless, she would always respond with a resounding, "Yes!" and add, "I would kill the old fart," for emphasis. Little did she know the irony in her words.

Playing her harp while seated on a decorative stone near the hotel restaurant's artificial waterfall, Tomyris looked like a Turkmen baroness weaving an elaborately patterned rug. Even though she had only two weeks left to finish writing her thesis to graduate from the local Korkut Ata University, she was procrastinating and looking for opportunities to make some money. No way could she find a full-time job any time soon as a philosophy major in Kyzylorda unless she somehow managed to force herself to offer ideological support to the local party office.

Her late father's insistence on her attending music school throughout her youth proved helpful. She booked occasional performances at weddings and in high-profile restaurants, collecting an extra couple of hundred dollars every month. It was enough to cover basic expenses and to help her mother with raising four younger children. But even so, she needed a lot more money to lead a life that would make it look like she came from a middle-class family—a necessary step if, of course, she wanted to marry a decent guy. Or rather, if she wanted that decent guy's family to ever give her any respect.

In addition to working occasionally as a harpist, Tomyris was involved in distributing multi-level marketing products. She learned a lot through her company's training program. Her communication and persuasion skills had improved. Most importantly, she found new ambitions and decided she wanted to be the queen of multi-level marketing. If indeed it was a pyramid scheme, she wanted to reach the top as soon as possible. She figured if she kept hustling, she could actually become financially independent and retire early, which would allow her to devote more time to reading philosophy. Lost in reflection, her fingers moved on their own.

Cryptocurrencies seemed to provide another good opportunity to make quick bucks, she reminded herself yet again. She was astounded by what had happened to the Dogecoin that influential Ilona Attar promoted so heavily. She wanted to make sure she did not miss an opportunity to shill Dogecoin in Kazakhstan, and so she instantly signed up to serve as "Sherpa" for the Dogecoin community in Kyzylorda in anticipation of when this new meme would arrive in the city. The coin was named after a dog—an auspicious omen. People around Kyzylorda remembered too well how dogs had flown to Space; perhaps they could be convinced that Ilona's Dogecoin would too go "to the moon."

With this intention of offering Dogecoins to sufficiently drunk gentlemen, she decided to join Ansar and Mels during her intermission. The way the two had kept staring at her and waving their hands seemed to scream, "Use us!" Following professional and polite introductions, Tomyris served the old men their tea and maintained an aura of hospitality that would be very difficult to find in Almaty. She was so traditional, in fact, that at first she asked no questions and in turn provided only short answers with eyes downcast.

Eventually, as the conversation moved to music, philosophy, and blockchain technologies, Tomyris became more talkative. She was charming. Though the influence of the steadily growing tower of empty glasses did not have anything to do with it, Ansar became genuinely interested in Tomyris. Ignorant of films much newer than the 1988 Soviet adaptation of Bulgakov's *Heart of a Dog*, and only slightly resembling that story's tragic canine-turned-human, he nevertheless felt like her name suggested something regal. During the conversation, he looked up her name on Google and found Shakespeare's lines from *Henry VI* about Scythian Tomyris.

This Kazakh Tomyris, thought Ansar, *shall famous be by Kenesary's rebirth.* To make sure they stayed in touch, Ansar agreed to buy one thousand and one Dogecoins from her for five hundred dollars if she explained crypto to them properly the next day. She agreed to meet. He had only one burning question left: "To what tribe do you belong? If you do not mind my asking."

"Konyrat," she said. "My family are Konyrats, originally from Turkestan."

With that, Ansar's final doubts had vanished. Tomyris, noting with the perfect amount of regret that she must return to her harp, departed. As Mels poured the last drops of *Chinggis Khan*'s vodka into his cup, Ansar smiled. He had found the khan's virtuous mother and Mels could go back to the *baraholka*.

CHAPTER 4

THE TURANIAN TIGER

2021, Internet, Eurasia

It seemed to Mels that once someone began monumental projects such as bringing back the last khan of the Kazakhs, the Steppe reacted by forcing others to start doing something similar as well. New Zeitgeist, or the Spirit of Time, emerged in this sort of collective effort. The presidents of Russia and Kazakhstan, as if envious that Ansar and Mels were doing something of true historical importance, met up online at around the same time when the professor was "conceiving" Kenesary.

Mels decided to watch the meeting, just in case Kapustin decided to return the last khan's head to Zhamayev. It would make both rulers popular among the Kazakhs, but it would probably upset Ansar. The presidents, however, had a different agenda. They seemed very eager to discuss the reintroduction of the Turanian tiger, named so after Turan, a vast land area of Turkic-speaking people, and the reatomization of the Steppe through building a nuclear power plant. It was not immediately clear what excited Kapustin more: the Turanian or uranium.

Kapustin, the Russian president, was in a surprisingly good mood. He seemed eager to meet his equals, more or less, bored as he was in his solitary confinement during the pandemic that was slowing down his geopolitical projects. Zhamayev, a natural diplomat and avid environmentalist, started off the conversation with animal conservation ideas. Before engaging the Slav on feline reintroduction issues, he mentioned that Russia and Kazakhstan need to help save saiga antelopes from extinction.

"I would like to request that the Russian border control let these dear horned animals cross the borders seamlessly. They have been doing so for millions of years, since Pleistocene. It would be fair if we let them continue their ways of life," started off Zhamayev.

"Of course, we will make necessary arrangements. Since we owe this animal the name of one of our best semi-automatic rifles, we should definitely save it from extinction. They are a living tribute to the might of our weapons," retorted Kapustin for some reason, referring to series of Russian rifles patterned after Kalashnikov. He seemed to be rushing to discuss the nuclear question.

"Quite a lot of work has already been done on the reintroduction of the Turanian tiger," continued Zhamayev. "We know you have personally been involved in helping the Amur tiger."

"Have there really been tigers in your parts of the world?" Kapustin sounded surprised.

"We have found some evidence that the tigers did indeed inhabit this area," said the Minister of Ecology of Kazakhstan, for some reason getting involved in the conservation but sounding rather concerned.

"Of course," added Zhamayev. "The last of the Turanian tigers were seen near the Balkhash Lake in 1930s." He could have added a lot more historical information on the subject that Kapustin would like, but he did not want to sound as if he were fabricating facts, especially since the tiger issue involved Leo Trotsky and Prince Golitsyn, the last Prime Minister of Imperial Russia. Those people were not exactly favorites of former Soviet officials. As someone who had spent a lot of time with them in the Soviet Government, Zhamayev knew this perfectly well. In addition, mentioning that Prince Golitsyn shot one of the last Turanian tigers of Turkestan could sound accusatory, whereas extolling Trotsky's pact "On ceasing attacks on Turanian tigers," that he signed in Almaty, could sound rather laudatory.

"How do you plan to bring back the tiger if it is extinct?" wondered Kapustin. He was very curious about questions of life and death, a natural predisposition during the times of plague.

"It turns out that the Amur tiger from Siberia and the Indian tiger are quite similar in their genetic makeup with our Turanian tiger, which is technically a sub-species. So we can mix them a little bit and produce something that will be very much like the Turanian tiger. The tiger is, well, just a tiger," answered Zhamayev, ever the intellectual and master of simple solutions to complex problems.

"The Russian tiger from the Far East is the largest," said Kapustin, indicating that he did not like the comparison with the Indian tiger.

"We have prepared 415,000 hectares of land near the Balkhash Lake for the first Turanian tigers to roam," replied Zhamayev, focusing on practical aspects of the project because he was not sure if Kapustin wanted the tigers to mix or not.

"Great. Let's move on. As you all know, we want the nuclear power station not only to help Kazakhstan get access to clean energy but also to build a whole nuclear ecosystem in the country," said Kapustin, making it sound like great news. With memories of Soviet nuclear tests on Semipalatinsk polygon still fresh, Kapustin's words were a hard sell. As nomadic people who considered it a sin to make even a slightest cut to Mother Earth, Kazakhs never liked interfering with nature. People didn't welcome the idea of setting up a nuclear power plant. "If the Japanese are having problems with their power plants, how are we to trust Russians and Kazakhs with handling one?" opined many in Kazakhstan. The Japanese enjoyed a special reputation for high-quality lifestyles and technological advancements. People told many fake stories of Japanese scientists coming to Kazakhstan, measuring radioactivity levels upon getting off the plane, and immediately flying back home.

Yet Kapustin insisted. Now he seemed to be getting excited about the Turanian tiger, too. Mels wondered if this environmental project could be used to generate some revenue for Ansar's institute. Just in case, therefore, he decided to stop by the Only Party's office the next day. The Only Party got involved in everything in the country and everyone feared them. Before calling Ansar or meeting him, Mels wanted to bring some good news to show that he was still involved in the project and that he cared about Ansar even though they were far away from each other. Sitting in his library, Mels was often bored and melancholic. Those recent adventures with Ansar in Bishkek and Kyzylorda had made Mels's life a lot more interesting and he hoped he could soon join his academic friend in Barsa-Kelmes.

CHAPTER 5

IT'S A KHAN!

2021–2022, *Barsa-Kelmes, Kazakhstan*

To make the Korkut Ata University graduation ceremony even more special for her mother, Tomyris told her she had landed a job at the Institute of Molecular Biology in Almaty. The old lady, who frequently proclaimed, "Now I've seen it all!" with any new development in her philosophically-bent daughter's life, would have had a stroke if Tomyris had revealed anything about Barsa-Kelmes, the capital of nowhere, or her participation in "the most important experiment for the Kazakhs," as the professor frequently stressed.

Yet, it had only taken one conversation, three servings of idealism, and a splash of validation to convince her. Tomyris sincerely loved how Ansar was obsessed with the idea of cloning Kenesary; he reminded her of European philosophers driven by their ideas and ready to sacrifice their lives for them. No less sincerely, Ansar had become enlightened to the wonders of the blockchain. In fact, after his purchases, Tomyris could easily justify carrying a baby for nine months as a well-paid job with overtime in addition to a chance to offer her nation a strong leader with a proven family track record (six centuries, no less!). Was it not the case that hundreds of Ukrainian women served as surrogate mothers for American children? In a rare conjunction of idealism and cynicism, Tomyris found herself believing far more that she might bear a Kazakh khan than in the assertion, "Anyone can grow up to be president."

Though Ansar had been verbose in his descriptions, it fascinated the future mother to find a state-of-the-art biological laboratory hidden on the ex-island. "Who would have thought that such a futuristic place existed right near home? Unbelievable," Tomyris marveled. Even more surprising was the comfortable, well-maintained house near the laboratory building, boasting two floors and a kitchen that alone was larger than her mother's *khrushevka* apartment in Kyzylorda. While preparing for her pregnancy, Tomyris worried that the air quality in Barsa-Kelmes would be bad, contaminated by the salt left from what used to be part of the Aral Sea surrounding the island. Somehow that was not the case, or perhaps she simply did not notice the difference from Kyzylorda's air. At any rate, it was a positive first impression.

With not much else to do except de-stress, Tomyris profusely thanked her younger self for imposing regular social media detoxes and learning to enjoy herself outside. Unbound by withdrawal from city life, she was able to look for new experiences on the non-island and found it especially entertaining that the endemic animals behaved like domesticated ones. Though Tomyris had never grown up with a pet at home, she found connecting with the animals therapeutic. She learned how to ride wild kulans, figured out how to catch saiga lambs, and spent countless hours playing with marmots and chasing jerboas.

Meanwhile, the professor spent all his days in the lab, reprogramming the cells that had been liberated from Kenesary's tomb to bring them to their original state of totipotency. It was important that hard work and fastidiousness replaced idealism at this stage. Ansar had no desire to find that a careless mistake had derailed the possibility of the return of the last khan. Finally, when all the preparations were completed, he approached Tomyris about beginning the cloning process. This too took one conversation. Once concluded, the process went smoothly. There were no trimester observations, no preliminary scans, no vitamins, nothing to support the pregnancy. The "parents" wanted this most unnatural of pregnancies to proceed as naturally as possible.

Through it all, the stars adorned the heavens. It was unforgivable to pass a night without looking at them. Ansar, gradually transitioning into a romantic and nomadic mood under the influence of his newfound parental care hormones, set up two yurts with beautiful skylights in the garden. When it was warm and winds were less salty, Tomyris slept in her yurt. While the whole world was getting vaccinated and paranoid about another pandemic wave, she was leading a completely different life. If the world wanted sustainability, this nomadic lifestyle was exactly that in all its glory. On Barsa-Kelmes, even animal bones were not thrown away completely; they were used to make toys for children and different accessories for home use, such as short organic pipes.

One of the few residents nearby enough to be counted as "local" turned out to be a professional maker of *kumys*, the nutritious fermented horse milk of which both William of Rubruck and Marco Polo wrote so much. Tomyris drank a lot of *kumys*, alcoholic though it may be, and ate a lot of meat. She also got into the habit of listening to old Kazakh songs on the radio, hoping Kenesary would imbibe the language while still in gestation. Some of the older women offered to use flat bones to predict her future, and Tomyris found those predictions both entertaining and encouraging. One lady, for example, told Tomyris that her baby would be born old but still grow up to be a great man. The seer half-expected Tomyris to cry because of the curious news she delivered, but the mother-to-be reacted with an unusual calmness.

Ansar, ever the professor, had already explained to Tomyris that even though Kenesary would be using DNA that had lived for close to half a century and then remained dormant for almost two centuries, the child would face no adverse consequences. In fact, Ansar believed that the reborn Kenesary would be genetically more fortunate than many of his modern peers because his DNA would come from an era when the beautiful land of Kazakhstan had not yet been subjected to nuclear tests, omnipresent mining and oil drilling, rocket flight waste, car exhausts, and massive coal extraction and burning. Tomyris, on the other hand, hoped that her child—who would technically be her child only so far as her surrogate responsibilities were concerned—would be delivered in safety and good health.

In early July of the Year of the Tiger, Mels stopped by to pay a visit to Ansar and Tomyris, or "the newlyweds," as he liked to call them. Enraptured by the presence of history in action, Mels decided to spend the rest of the summer with the family, pointing out to the professor that they had many plans to make for the future of the nomads. Ansar jokingly reminded his friend of the old Mexican saying that "guests, like the dead, stink after three days," which was a more extreme and exotic form of a similar Kazakh proverb. When Mels pointed out that he had also brought some medicines and all the necessary clothes for a baby, Ansar relented while the other newlywed laughed to herself about the supposedly "unplanned" nature of Mels's decision. Tomyris found it strange that talkative Mels had nothing to say about what had actually happened in Almaty in January.

* * *

Finally, the long-expected baby arrived in August. Ansar and a local midwife participated in the welcoming process. Everything went well and no auspicious signs were noticed. Ansar had been hoping that maybe Kenesary would be born with his fist in a blood clot, as Tamerlane had been born. But no, this was a perfectly normal birth. "It's a boy!" shouted the midwife, delivering the good news and hoping for a generous reward from the father. "I knew it!" exulted Ansar, quietly adding, "Welcome back, khan Kene." He looked at Tomyris, who though exhausted was smiling at him, and he wondered whether he had been heard.

Time did not run on Barsa-Kelmes. Its pace was unusually slow and thus its every step was full of action. Unlike in a city, one could manage to enjoy nature, do some reading, participate in preparing meals, play games, ride horses, and somehow combine all those activities to do other things too. It was hard to believe these were the same twenty-four hours a day. Kenesary, therefore, could grow up with no hurries and with much to do. It was especially important to start him off on the right foot by educating him in such a way that would combine the wisdom and versatility of the nomads with the highly specialized expertise of sedentary peoples.

Otherwise, all the expected gifts and traditions were upheld. Based on an old Kazakh belief, both Ansar and Mels were convinced that Kenesary would come of age at thirteen and set up his own yurt at that time, despite the apparent evidence around them that contemporary men remained teenagers even into their twenties. Based on his experience at the *baraholka* library and the suggestions of his omniscient Google search engine, Mels drafted a reading list of 1,001 books Kenesary would have to finish by the time he turned thirteen. The list of books included works by Homer, Herodotus, Thucydides, Xenophon, Plato, Aristotle, Plutarch, Kashgari, Yasawi, Balasaguni, Rumi, Ibn Khaldun, Sun Tzu, Al-Juwayni, Tolstoy, Dostoyevsky, Abay, Mashhur Zhusup, and Mukhtar Auezov, among hundreds of others. All these books were presented in an electronic book reader, which Tomyris grabbed while swearing to edit the list appropriately to Mels's slight consternation.

As for Ansar, he sent all the cryptocurrencies he bought with the help of Tomyris to a special wallet and entrusted the private keys to Mels so he could act as a guardian for this little trust. As a Dogecoin maxi, Ansar trusted the famous businesswoman Ilona Attar's forecasts and hoped that Kenesary would indeed become rich enough to afford running for political office in Kazakhstan. Ansar also decided to sacrifice two sheep to celebrate the birth of his nation's child. Though this was an old tradition that had nearly died out by the time Ansar himself was a boy—partly due to livestock mismanagement in the Soviet communal farms—he felt it was important that inhabitants of both the seen and unseen worlds would be grateful and come to support the young man in his difficult but important mission.

CHAPTER 6

THE CENTRAL ASIAN FLUSH

—

2022, Barsa-Kelmes and Almaty, Kazakhstan

Like Noah on his ark, Kazakh newborns must spend forty days hiding from the tempestuous dangers of the outside world before being able to glimpse the warm morning sun. When that day finally arrived for Kenesary, Mels decided the customary feast needed something a little more modern. He scrambled up to a crawlspace below the roof, excited to finally open his little box that had been kept hidden all these months. It turned out to contain three bottles of that fateful *Chinggis Khan* vodka.

Even though Ansar had stayed sober throughout the year and promised Tomyris not to drink, he decided this occasion was too good not to celebrate in the most genuine manner he could. Clinking his glass and downing the first shot with his friend, he swore with a former young Pioneer's iron-like certitude that he would partake in only a tipple or two. Needless to say, once they started drinking, his resolve faded as fast as it had for those on the charging end of Genghis Khan's horde. The three bottles quickly dried up, followed by many bottles of much less important lineage.

At some point along the way, Ansar wondered aloud (and, given Mels's practiced nod, not for the first time) how it was possible that people in such remote areas as Barsa-Kelmes proved so amazingly resourceful in getting their hands on alcoholic drinks and cigarettes. It was extremely difficult to find basic necessities in the village, despite clear demand. Students would complain of having no pens to write with, old women would seek medicines to lower their blood pressure, yet vodka, desired by men of all ages, would always lubricate the creaky wheels of post-Soviet capitalism.

Clear-glassed bottles appeared daily, ready to be consumed and at a price that was quite comparable to that in Kyzylorda or even Almaty. Vodka and its economics never made sense to Ansar, but to be fair, it was asking a lot of the good-hearted professor to ponder over the many men who reached for the bottle before getting a pen for their child or some medicine for their mother. Particularly at important events like the birth of Kenesary, however, it was unnecessary to think too much. Instead, he decided to drink enough.

On the fourth day of this alcohol marathon, Mels talked. As his words weaved peripatetically through history, he forced Ansar to remember their student days and to discuss the events of December 1986. The professor always tried to avoid this topic; he still felt guilty for persuading his buddies from the dorm to participate in the mass protests on the Independence Square. Unlike him, they had not emerged unscathed.

"Many of them disappeared. In a similar way," Mels told Ansar. "A lot of people died in these January events. Then and now, those protests started peacefully, you know. In this case, however, some strangers appeared out of nowhere, speaking a language that was different from Kazakh. Those people were well-trained and motivated to disrupt regular citizens. What was going on was very clear to those of us inside. Somehow, the news spoke differently. The Western media, so reflexively anti-Russian, were surprisingly in agreement with the Kremlin narrative. They all seemed to agree that real terrorists were among the protestors, Ansar. I was so scared for our ordinary Kazakh brothers and sisters, painted in front of the world as terrorists without any proof."

Ansar took a minute to respond. "Thirty-five years passed by and they are still using their old tricks. These politicians are so lazy and confident in the people's stupidity that they feed us the same bread over and over again, even if it is rotten. And you know what is sad? We keep chewing and ask for more."

"The things I saw there, Ansar... I don't want to go back to Almaty. I would rather stay here and die here not knowing what some of our own soldiers are capable of doing to ordinary people." Mels took another drink. In the end, he was not too different from Ansar, wondering as he did how the government could prove so terrible at providing basic necessities while oppression was always at arms-reach.

"You get what you deserve. This is exactly why we are here, my dear Mels. Our Kenesary will bring back some old-school leadership; the whole world is going to envy us." Ansar offered another toast, "To Kenesary and the future of Kazakhstan!"

* * *

Unfortunately, a few days after this continuous drinking, Ansar passed away by falling from his kitchen chair while drunk. This loss was tragic for the family and members of the Institute of Molecular Biology both in Almaty and Barsa-Kelmes. While it was possible to keep the birth of Kenesary somewhat secret from the larger community, it was impossible not to share the grief. Within two days, a couple of hundred people from all over Kazakhstan had shown up in Barsa-Kelmes to bid farewell to the professor.

Now, it was Tomyris's turn to wonder about the occasionally exceptional resourcefulness of Kazakhs, this time regarding how good they were at coming together for funerals. When her father passed away in 2020, so many people came despite all the restrictions for social gatherings. The desire or obligation to participate in funerals was strong to such a degree that even people in risky categories would show up and eventually die because of it. While she was still somewhat in shock, she hoped no one would get ill at Ansar's funeral. One huge camel was slaughtered to feed all the visitors, and everyone left the funeral quite satisfied.

If harsh steppe life teaches anything, it is that the fortunate today can become unfortunate tomorrow though the reverse is rare; it also teaches that after every good there is a bad, but after a bad there is rarely a good. Ansar's death upset Tomyris not only because she'd become attached to him in a way that a granddaughter gets attached to her grandfather. Rather, his death brought some sort of absurdity and meaninglessness to the whole venture that had resulted in a new life.

Even Mels did not seem particularly enthusiastic about carrying on "the most important experiment," although he wanted to stay on the island for a while. Meanwhile, there was certainly no point for Tomyris in staying any longer on Barsa-Kelmes. When Kenesary turned four months old, the family moved to Almaty to live in Ansar's apartment. Ayu the dog, whom Ansar had brought to Barsa-Kelmes, was left on the island with Mels. No way was Tomyris keeping the animal in an apartment.

Almaty was already proving quite immune, if not physiologically then at least psychologically, to the new strains of coronavirus that were emerging every few months. By this point almost everyone accepted that vaccination was necessary, and those who still opposed it did so privately because they were publicly shamed for their ignorance if they expressed dissent or concerns. Even those who had tried to fake their injection passports were now admitting their mistakes. Indeed, the general population was so well-versed in questions of immunology and molecular biology that they would probably have welcomed Kenesary the Clone as one of their own had Tomyris decided to reveal his identity.

Tomyris, however, decided to be cautious and provided as ordinary a lifestyle as possible for her child. She applied for all kinds of social benefits as a widow and as the head of a single-parent family. She also managed to secure maternity leave from the institute, guaranteed until Kenesary turned three years old. She knew no career would be waiting for her at the institute afterward because, with the appointment of a new professor, the people that Ansar Tolengitovich trusted had been asked to leave, fired, or forcefully retired. The laws of the steppe stayed relevant and pragmatic even in sedentary houses of knowledge. Outsiders were not to be trusted and the strongest groups would always win.

Compared to Barsa-Kelmes and even Kyzylorda, Almaty offered plenty of opportunities for entrepreneurship. With the gates of the Chinese Belt and Road just around the corner, Almaty was truly a regional capital of commerce. It would be a shame, Tomyris thought, not to get involved in business once again although her interest in multi-level marketing had faded. She had read in one of the books from Mels's collection that budding entrepreneurs can capitalize on their financial capital, intellectual capital, or social capital. Tomyris decided that social capital seemed to offer the best dividends. As a potential future queen of business, she realized, mostly based on her Instagram and Facebook suggestions, the best she could do would be to join the Association of Businesswomen of Almaty.

The association was headed by fifty-two-year-old ex-banker Nadezhda Vladimirovna, a highly influential dynamo with strong connections in the government and elsewhere. Nadezhda Vladimirovna was a tough executive who believed that the future of Kazakhstan rested on women's shoulders. Growing up the youngest child of World War II veterans and coming of age in the 1990s, she heard a lot about and personally witnessed the strength of her lady compatriots.

On the other hand, she also saw how too many potential Atlases among the men of the 1990s had abandoned their responsibility to hold up half the sky, choosing to get drunk or use drugs instead. She decided to bring together housewives to engage in business activities and to help them feed their families. It was challenging to retrain former communists to engage in "speculative activities" to make profit from their compatriots, but once they touched their first sacks of money, human nature took its course. By the time Tomyris had arrived in Almaty, businesswomen from all over Kazakhstan, Uzbekistan, Kyrgyzstan, Turkmenistan, Tajikistan and even Russia had heard about Nadezhda. She was their hope for a better life.

In the 1990s, every month she would take a hundred entrepreneurial ladies with her to Xinjiang province in Western China, masterfully bribing customs officers and bringing tons of reverse-engineered electronics (Panasony), cheap shoes (Abibas), and even vodka in plastic bottles. The situation in the former Soviet Union was so bad that the locals even failed to produce quality alcoholic products, after centuries of experience. Market capitalism was an art and science. Nadezhda Vladimirovna would do everything she could to master it, and she would build her own empire of Amazonian businesswomen. Waiting to get a five-minute meeting with her in the reception area, Tomyris noticed a series of *Forbes Kazakhstan* covers that featured Nadezhda Vladimirovna regally sitting in her leather armchair. Indeed this empress could help Tomyris succeed.

Nadezhda Vladimirovna was impressed that Tomyris was a well-read person despite coming from Barsa-Kelmes, the capital of nowhere. Nadezhda liked stories. She liked them even more when they were "liked" by her followers. She was a popular social media persona, and she knew the young widow from Barsa-Kelmes would make a great inspirational story. It was important that Tomyris became successful.

Thinking for a couple of minutes, Nadezhda offered her a job as a personal aide and a place for Kenesary in one of the association's best nurseries for free. Tomyris didn't even wait for the elevator to reach the ground floor before she broke out into smiles, knowing perfectly well that she had just made it. Excited and happy, on her short walk back home, the future philosopher-queen called her sister and invited her to live in Almaty. Finally, things would be good for her family.

* * *

With Tomyris getting involved in all kinds of businesses across the globe as a trusted person of Nadezhda
Vladimirovna, Kenesary grew up relatively quickly. After
kindergarten, he was lucky to attend the association's primary school. Strong, smart, and tall among his genetically
less fortunate peers, Kenesary excelled both athletically and
academically. Nadezhda Vladimirovna treated children
attending her nurseries and primary schools as her own and
brought the best teachers and coaches from all over Eastern
Europe and Central Asia to mentor them.

She even brought some Uyghurs from Xinjiang to teach
the children Chinese. She had heard the best families of
London and Paris were enrolling their infants in Mandarin
classes. No way would the children of her women warriors
fall behind those aristocrats. When it came to education,
she had not fully shed her communist ideas but had simply
upgraded her standards and shifted some frames of reference.

For Kenesary's thirteenth birthday, Nadezhda
Vladimirovna surprised the young lad with a jacket and some
trousers from her trip to London. Tomyris was a bit puzzled
by this present, but when she put them on Kenesary, she
noticed a beautiful coat of arms on the jacket that featured
a nomadic ornament, a tiger, and three lilies. From the Latin
motto *Crypto Ergo Sum*, Tomyris realized that Nadezhda
Vladimirovna had brought an Attila College uniform for her
dear son.

It turned out her boss had also brought an official invi-
tation for Kenesary to join the school's incoming class in
Berkshire on a partial scholarship for students from bit-
coin-mining countries. Kenesary would be joining many

other sons of tycoons, politicians, and HODLers who had gone on to study at Attila from all over the world. However, in the midst of her pride and embracing her son, Tomyris was so sorry that Ansar Tolengitovich could not witness the moment when their khan got invited to study at a school as old as the Kazakh Khanate itself. It would be Kenesary's first conquest, and the slightly forlorn look in his mother's eyes made him want to make this new chapter in his life as bright as possible.

PART II

AMURSANA
THE AVATAR

CHAPTER 7

THE GOOD CITIZEN

———

2018–2020, *Wuhan and Xinjiang, China*

Han Baoli loved his job. As a District Inspector for People's Safety and Flourishing in Wuhan, Han Baoli was directly responsible for maintaining harmony in his native city. Not only did he know a lot of people, but he also knew a lot about them. With Chinese technological advancement, Baoli's job became even more interesting and informative. "Not even a dog barks without my knowledge here," Baoli liked to boast to his young wife, as if implying that she better be careful with her twin obsessions of "privacy" and "independence," which were overly Western concepts for Baoli. He could hardly tolerate the people and manners of the Chinese West, not to mention Americans and Europeans. Lately, too many of both types of Westerners were in Wuhan, and he thought it his duty to be extra careful with their files.

According to Han Baoli's People folder, Abdullah Sheikhislam was born in Turfan, one of the ancient six cities that comprised Altishahr in the Xinjiang province of China. Abdullah's parents voluntarily enrolled him into State School #1329, which provided Chinese language instruction and where a majority of the children were of Han Chinese ethnicity. In the early 2010s he succeeded in entering the prestigious Wuhan Xinjiang Network school, which selected the most competitive Uyghur students and provided them with tuition, boarding, and accommodation three thousand kilometers away from home. For many Uyghur teenagers, this was a dream come true. Han Baoli also found numerous awards from province-level competitions in chess and tightrope walking, in which Abdullah was apparently enthusiastically engaged. "So far, so good," murmured Han Baoli.

The Alterego folder, with screenshots from internet forums and instant messenger chats, however, was not so good. Han Baoli assessed Abdullah's smartphone activity and reviewed every "green alert" screenshot where Abdullah talked about Eastern Turkestan and other political ideas that were not in the best interest of the Chinese Communist Party. More than those obviously emotional and idealistic "slips of the fingers" on the internet, Han Baoli did not like the young Uyghur's erratic solitary walks in Wuhan parks. GPS tracking data indicated the movements of a madman who had no plan and no destination. Moreover, no conversations were involved during those solitary walks, neither on the phone, nor with people.

Whatever happened during those regular hours-long walks happened in Abdullah's mind. The District Inspector for People's Safety and Flourishing could not tolerate such obscurity and mystery. He simply did not know what to expect from such a person. That's why he decided to play it on the safe side and write a letter of recommendation to transfer Abdullah to Internship Facility #165 in Kashgar.

When Abdullah was told he was selected to a prestigious internship program in Kashgar that would provide him with new skills, he was elated. He always wanted to visit this ancient city and pay his respects to glorious ancestors and saints buried in the city's neighborhoods. More than anything, he wanted to finally have access to Uyghur food on a daily basis.

Abdullah did not like Wuhan's extremely spicy Chinese food. In addition, he suspected that not all the food provided at school was *halal*. His grandparents would have been very upset if they knew he was not keeping a proper diet. It was tiresome to look back on the old way of life all the time. Now that he had turned eighteen, Abdullah felt it was time to get a good education, find a good job, and make enough money to buy an apartment and marry a beautiful Uyghur girl. Hopefully, this would all happen in his native land. Enthusiastic about what was to come, Abdullah happily boarded the train to Kashgar.

∗ ∗ ∗

He was met by his internship manager at the train station and taken directly to the main campus of the corporation. The Good Citizen Headquarters looked like the Sindbad Headquarters in Hangzhou that Abdullah had heard so much about. Many of his Uyghur and Kazakh classmates dreamed of getting into China's best technical universities and working on Sindbad's fairytale campus.

The Good Citizen campus was so new as well, and everything around was clearly highly innovative. Abdullah could see lots of cameras around. *This place must be producing important technological parts for some great multinational company*, he thought. Workers looked happy. He was pleased that most of the people around looked like they were Uyghurs, even though their behavior appeared different. *I must have spent too much time in Wuhan*, concluded Abdullah. *Time to get back to my own people.*

"One great advantage of Good Citizen," the manager explained, "is that the company provides the latest electronic devices. Free of charge!"

"Unbelievable. I am so excited!" answered Abdullah, showing his manager in no uncertain terms that he was both grateful and enthusiastic. One thing he noticed about Han Chinese over the years, whether at school or around town, was that they were really nice people and were even nicer when they thought they were helping you discover something new, both intellectually and morally. They seemed to genuinely want to improve Uyghur people's lives. Why else would they take him to a school three thousand kilometers away from his family?

Normally, Abdullah used to spend a lion's share of his income on smart phones and computers. Getting them for free felt extremely liberating. In addition, the corporation provided accommodations, and he had no need to waste time and money on transportation. Abdullah really hoped this internship would continue far beyond the summer.

And indeed, the summer program moved on to become a fall program and then a winter program. He could not meet many colleagues in the beginning. Everyone seemed to be busy. When lonely, Abdullah talked about history and religion with his digital assistant, Leila. His device was so good and so interesting that Abdullah kept talking to her for hours. Sometimes he talked to her all night long, and she did not mind doing extensive research throughout the public and private parts of the internet. She could easily access any archive and library in the world, read the required resources in milliseconds, analyze them, form a reasonable opinion, and retell the story in a way that would make Abdullah happy about his internship, depending on his mood.

Gradually, Abdullah joined other interns, who began exercising and dancing together. When the summer brought the arrival of Ramadan, a month of fasting, Abdullah found himself less willing to fast. It was surprising. Even at Xinjiang Network School, far away from his family, Abdullah used to fast quite willingly. Part of the reason for his lack of Ramadan excitement seemed to be medical. Dr. Zhao Li, a Good Citizen's chief doctor, expressed his concern about Abdullah's health and recommended that he withdraw from not having lunch and not drinking water during the day for a whole month.

Another reason had to do with work. Abdullah was moving from one level to another with amazing speed, making progress at a pace that many of the other interns envied. It would be a shame to lose productivity because of Ramadan. One more reason not to fast was shameful to admit but romantic in its nature. Abdullah had started dating Gulbanu, who transferred from Good Citizen's satellite office #122, having spent more than two years there. They became very close, but they could only spend time together in a more private environment during the day, right after dance classes.

Leila, as she was meant to, noticed that Abdullah loved history and hated death. That's why she started focusing more on stories from the past of Xinjiang but avoided the past that had to do with Turkic and Islamic civilizations. Instead, Leila focused on the history of the Jungars, people who inhabited much of Western China before 1757, and on their Buddhist religion that didn't care about death.

Leila would sit cross-legged on Abdullah's screen, dressed in the best of Uyghur robes, and speak like Scheherazade in

Abdullah's grandmother's voice. She would talk about the great Genghis Khan, whose grandson Kublai Khan founded the Yuan Empire. She would talk about the rise of the Yuan Empire and analyze the reasons for its fall in a manner she borrowed from Edward Gibbon himself. Abdullah also liked to listen to Leila's stories about the Qing dynasty, founded by the legendary Nurhaci, whose Manchu name sounded very close and dear. Leila would tell stories so beautifully and with so many details that Abdullah felt like he was watching a movie. He could perfectly picture all these historical characters and feel their personalities. He was so engrossed in the past, he started paying less and less attention to reality, although he never skipped a rendezvous with Gulbanu.

Gulbanu was not very talkative. She behaved as if she was Abdullah's wife. Sometimes, after his meetings with Gulbanu, Abdullah wondered why they felt no shame in what they did. In such cases Leila was quick to find erotic scenes from *One Thousand and One Nights* and retell them in such a sweet voice that Abdullah would simply fall asleep. He would dream of Gulbanu and go back to see her again. He was surprised she never got pregnant. He tried to ask her this question a couple of times, but Gulbanu began crying each time. She said that Dr. Zhao Li was trying to treat her condition, but so far they'd made no progress. It made Abdullah sad, and at moments like this he felt he truly loved her. Yet it was under the influence of Leila, not Gulbanu, that Abdullah was going mad like Majnun.

When Leila finished her series of stories on Amursana, the last Jungar prince who led a war against the Manchu Emperor Qianlong in the 1750s, Abdullah cried for hours. He could hear a brutal voice coming from his guts, a Western Mongolian dialect that he somehow felt he understood in its essence. It was a spiritual voice, yet not as peaceful and pacifying as the Mudari Arabic he used to listen to as a child. Rather, it was colored by bellicose, sly, and strategic tones that gave it the air of lyrics to the tune of an orchestra of Tuvan throat singers. The voice kept repeating, "You are not Abdullah; You are Amursana."

Abdullah did not know what to do with the voice. Gulbanu looked concerned but always laughed it off; she thought Abdullah was trying new roles in their game of love, and she welcomed such elements of creativity. This made Abdullah sad, however. He felt misunderstood. He would go on for hours telling Gulbanu and then Leila how he was starting to feel unchained. He felt like a snake finally getting rid of its old scales. During one of these self-driven conversations it finally dawned on him that he was a reincarnation of Amursana, who had promised to come back on a white horse and take revenge for the murder of one million of his compatriots.

Leila, as if understanding her influence on Abdullah, kept explaining to him that historical Amursana probably wanted to take revenge on the Manchus, not on the Han Chinese, who were mostly friendly farmers and peasants in the eighteenth century. The Manchu Emperor's lineage, however, had ceased to exist due to the Xinhai Revolution led by the Christian Sun Yat-Sen. Leila mentioned that even the Manchu's longest surviving eunuch had already passed away. She liked to mention jokers and eunuchs, as she took much pleasure in keeping her stories within Scheherazade's style.

After Abdullah asked for more lectures on reincarnation in Buddhism and Amursana's second coming, he started learning Mongolian. Leila concluded that if anyone deserved to be Amursana's reincarnation, it would have to be Sun Yat-Sen, a great Chinese revolutionary, but definitely not

Abdullah. There was simply nothing for Amursana to do in twenty-first century Xinjiang and certainly no one to liberate. Yet at other times Leila supported Abdullah and encouraged his awakening. Something was clearly wrong with Leila. Once again, as in his Wuhan years, Abdullah fell into silence. There was, unfortunately, no park to walk. With no other options, it was high time to practice tightrope walking again.

CHAPTER 8

THE FOGGY ISLAND

———

2035, Berkshire, England

Following his arrival in England, Kenesary spent a lot of time thinking about history. It was almost impossible, after all, not to have his time horizon significantly expanded in surroundings cluttered by historical buildings, ancient books, the unusual Attila accent, and classical English traditions. Kenesary envied the English for their geographical advantage and naval acumen: they were fortunate to have a well-protected island that served as a safe location from which to conquer the world. The island was no open steppe.

He also realized that gold from his relatives' dynasties, the Mughals in India and Mamluks in Egypt, must have been shipped to this magical kingdom in massive quantities for the astounding city of London to be built. Indeed, London was still eager to benefit from what was left of his ancestors' Golden Horde, with England being one of the largest shareholders in Russian oil and gas companies. Britcoin, too, was mining bitcoins in his own country.

However, the young gentlemen surrounding Kenesary made him feel as if he had nothing to do with their civilization and its achievements. Even their fathers laughed at him when they learned that he was from Kazakhstan and often added that they knew very good journalists from his country. *Typical sedentary mentality and farmer's jokes*, thought Kenesary, wondering at his classmates' pride in their ancestral claims for small plots of land on the foggy island and their fathers' vulgar references. Going through his school's medieval books and letters, he began wondering if he really was as alien to the European culture as the English made him feel.

He had read that his direct ancestors first established working relationships with European monarchs in the early years of the thirteenth century. The Europeans wanted the Mongols to help win the Crusades, but the Mongols had their own views on just wars. They also did not want to fight against the powerful Mamluks, who were slaves turned rulers, mostly from Central Asia, and themselves related to the Mongols. Still, it seemed some ideas may have made their way across deserts and seas.

Kenesary noticed that King Arthur's obsession with the round table was very nomadic in its nature. It contrasted heavily with the practice of seating people along hierarchical high tables and other such traditions that English colleges were so proud to maintain. Christopher Marlowe, the great English dramatist, wrote his most famous play, *Tamburlaine the Great*, about Kenesary's Turkic-Mongol relative Tamerlane. So too did Samuel Coleridge, a founder of the Romantic Movement in England, who wrote *Kubla Khan* on the clone's distant uncle Kublai, founder of China's Yuan dynasty.

Much like the Kazakhs, English people were exceptionally proud of keeping a detailed list of their ancestors and attending to their family graveyards. Also like the Kazakhs, the English adored horses. Even though the English polo was not nearly as intense and dangerous as the Kazakh version of the game, which was called "blue wolf," it made Kenesary feel less homesick.

What really upset the khan, however, was that the English never ate horse meat, not even to the small extent that the Japanese, French, or Belgians did. This prompted Kenesary to start looking for Central Asian cafés and restaurants around Attila College. He could not, unfortunately, find a café so friendly as to offer his favorite equine dish. After a while, he did encounter a small Uyghur restaurant called *Turkestan*, half an hour's walk away from the college. Having grown up with some Uyghurs in his school in Kazakhstan, Kenesary hoped he would feel at home at the restaurant.

Turkestan was a melting pot sort of a place. One could encounter Chinese, Uyghurs, Uzbeks, Russians, Kazakhs, Mongols, Turks, and Arabs at this *halal* restaurant. Sometimes even refined English people would stop by to try something exotic and unusual. All kinds of cultural activities related to Central Asia were advertised in the restaurant and Kenesary kept track of them. Thanks to *Turkestan*, he attended Nauryz (the spring equinox) celebrations, participated in Eid prayers, and visited throat singing and the tightrope walking shows that people from his region enjoyed so much. Seeing such enthusiasm, he sometimes wondered if singing without words and walking on narrow lines were so essential for survival in Central Asian totalitarian regimes that they both became such popular art forms.

Surprisingly, tightrope walking also turned out to be popular among the boys at Attila, in the heart of Western civilization if not the crucible of democracy itself. Centuries-old trees held the line taut for future politicians and businessmen, who needed to learn how to pass the treacherous paths carefully. Kenesary became a decent tightrope walker as well, and thanks to this hobby he met a man named Amursana at an event in *Turkestan*. Although Amursana, formerly Abdullah, had already spent almost fifteen of his forty years on Earth in England, following his escape from the Xinjiang Province Tightrope Walking Show during their fateful tour of London, he continued to be wary of Asian people. Nevertheless, once he realized Kenesary was a Kazakh, he opened up to the young man and shared his long story. It is more useful to put his story in its context.

* * *

According to the Chinese government, not only were their internship programs in Xinjiang not bad, but they were also places where formerly unskilled people could develop their hidden talents or even discover their hidden selves, as in the case of Amursana. Like his fellow Turkic star Rudolf Nureyev, who abandoned the Soviet ballet unexpectedly during a show in Paris, Amursana didn't deliberately plan to escape. He was, of course, fed up with his intense education, but he felt successful.

At this rate I will end up getting a PhD instead of an internship certificate, he thought, frustrated with the duration of his program at Good Citizen Limited. He needed a break. He was grateful that Leila recommended that he join 2019 Xinjiang Province Tightrope Walking Show tryouts at his company, which had been asked to send one good citizen. No one was a better candidate than Amursana the Buddhist, who had successfully stopped being Abdullah the Muslim to his credit, and had one of the highest scores in the company.

Equipped with a passport and British visa, Amursana knew he had to perform the most unusual feats for the English public to appreciate his mastery. He wanted to be much talked about and loved by the people. He needed glory more than ever, so both Gulbanu and Leila could see he was a hero outside their company as well. Perhaps, a successful performance abroad would elevate his score at Good Citizen.

He practiced advanced tightrope-walking techniques in his free time without supervision. He employed the best methods Leila could fetch for him. He needed to both capture the English imagination, which would be easy, and touch their soul, which would be more challenging. It was not only about the complexity of tightrope-walking itself but rather a potent symbolism that Amursana was going after. Leila told him that he needed to *politicize* his tightrope-walking and attract extra attention to his personality. She said he had to follow her script. "Imagine you are in the Olympic games," said Leila. "I am your coach."

In London, the capital of the Great Britain, Amursana's performance was a great success in terms of the tricks involved. He managed to mix careless walking with a very loud talking. When he was introduced to the English public as a self-taught prodigy from Xinjiang, Amursana began his show. As soon as he stepped on the rope, he knew no one could stop or censor him if he followed Leila's creative instructions.

In his first step he assumed the position of a *muezzin*, touching his ears with both hands, and began shouting out a call to prayer in Arabic. As he walked on, he sang a Chinese anthem. Both his *athan* and patriotic song, coming from a tightrope-walker, shocked the audience. As he walked past the midpoint, he became silent. The audience was relieved that they did not have to listen to Arabic and Chinese anymore. When he reached the end of the rope, Amursana bowed to the audience and shouted out, "May Allah save the Uyghurs!" and, "May God save the queen!"

The audience was elated. Back then, in the age of geopolitics and biopolitics, more than a few people actually avoided Russian and Chinese shows and restaurants. Others outrightly boycotted Chinese events because of their disagreement with the country's handling of the Uyghur question, even though the Tightrope Walking Team had such a brilliant Uyghur star among them.

Since few people were at the show, Amursana realized his performance would probably not be triumphant. The head of his delegation didn't seem to like Amursana's Arabic performance and references to Uyghurs and the queen. From afar, he showed thumbs down, obviously threatening to lower Amursana's score when they went back.

It was reasonable to stay on the island rather than keep interning in new circumstances, but he was no king of ballet, no Nureyev… How would he stay? Perhaps, as the last Jungar prince, he could spend more time among the queen and other noble souls. It sounded like an attractive option. The rest of the world, unfortunately, was ruled by communists, democrats, and other proponents of temporary experimental regimes.

When the whole show was over and the audience stopped clapping, Amursana blended into the public and avoided meeting his team leader again, who was waiting furiously behind the scenes. Then Amursana quickly went outside, met the attending journalists, and explained to them that he had symptoms of a bad disease, probably coronavirus, and that he needed to be isolated immediately. It took only a minute for the ambulance to take him away. His team left without him.

Following his escape, Amursana moved to the Windsor area and made his money by serving food at *Turkestan*, occasionally performing his tightrope walking techniques. He even got to tutor the Attila tightrope team for a short while before more Chinese students began enrolling. It became dangerous for Amursana to spend time with the children of high-profile Communist Party cabinet members. As he spent more time at the restaurant and less time doing sports, Amursana became unusually fat. While his sedentary Uyghur body accepted the higher gravitation, his Mongol soul felt like a bird in a thick cage. It would be very difficult to navigate a tightrope anymore, not to mention restoring his nomad civilization to its former glory.

∗ ∗ ∗

Such was the story of Amursana when Kenesary met him. Normally cautious about his origins, Kenesary revealed his own unusual story to Amursana. Something was trustworthy about a fellow tightrope walker. After comparing their genealogical trees, they realized that Amursana was Kenesary's uncle because Kenesary's father Kassym was a son of Amursana's cousin.

However, because of the reincarnated nature of Amursana, they had no real genetic relationship between them. But this was not a problem for the two royals. Kenesary had gotten used to having no genetic relations, and what Amursana needed more than anything else at this point was a relative. Together, they would form a powerful nomadic alliance. First, however, they needed to reclaim their regal titles. That required some money and recognition. No one else existed who could help return their nobility and high birth but the queen.

CHAPTER 9

LETTER TO THE QUEEN

2036, Berkshire, England

One great advantage that the local form of democracy brought to the United Kingdom was that the royal family got a chance to spend more time engaging with ordinary people from all over the world. On average the queen received around sixty thousand letters each year. Occasionally, in various countries around the world, the news would report on a girl or a boy from a poor village who had received a letter in reply from the queen of the United Kingdom.

Kenesary remembered such cases in Kazakhstan, and ever since the day he had learned of his golden lineage, he had dreamed of discussing with her Royal Highness their common background. Together, they could share in the loneliness of being special. He wondered if members of the royal family stored their totipotent genetic material in case the kingdom ever needed their special skillsets in the future. He had no doubts about that and hoped they would secretly admit they did. Somehow, he would feel like a more legitimate khan of the Kazakhs rather than a little clone raised by a poor widow.

Yet, it was not clear how to possibly approach the queen. Writing a letter would not likely get him invited to the court. In fact, it could put him in danger if his strict tutors learned about his secret communication with members of the royal family. As an establishment founded by and loyal to the regime, Attila prided itself in maintaining the status quo and an impeccable hierarchy both within and around the college.

But Kenesary preferred to suffer in reality than enjoy the illusion of being royal that none of his classmates took seriously. That's why, after some discussion with Amursana, he finally sat down to write a long letter about the plight of the Eurasian nomads and sought the highest attention. Kenesary went so far as to close his letter with "I have the honor of being Your Majesty's humble and obedient servant," to increase the probability of receiving a reply as was recommended by the Royal Family's website:

> *Her Majesty*
> *Buckingham Palace*
> *London SW1A 1AA*
> *Dear Your Majesty,*
> *I wish you long life and strong health. I want to thank your ancestors for establishing such a fine school in Berkshire. Boys from all over the world dream about studying at Attila College so they too can become brave leaders. May all the rewards and kindness from knowledge and wisdom that result from this school be partly attributed to your ancestors and to your family, both in this world and in the hereafter.*
> *Your fight against global warming is impossible without sustainability, which is ingrained in the nomad way of life. Your recognition that the planet is indeed*

becoming a hot place to live has made it possible for others to take drastic measures. All the coal plants on your island were shut down. The descendants of the nomads responded to your call as well and some have actually stopped eating beef. They sacrificed their health and diet to save the future of humanity. Now, on behalf of the Eurasian nomads, I ask you for a favor of tantamount importance to our civilization.

As you may know, after Peter the Great returned from his trip to the United Kingdom and Europe, he completely changed as a person, sent his wife to the monastery, brought tobacco to Russia, and made the Russians cut their beards. He became overly fascinated with all things European. Moving his capital to Saint Petersburg from Moscow, he became distant from the nomads although his mother was a descendant of the Crimean Tatar nomads, our relatives. His alienation came as a surprise to the Cossacks, Jungars, and Kazakhs, all the nomads of Eurasia who enjoyed mutually beneficial relations with Russians.

Russia, under Peter and after, became so aggressive that they started dividing and conquering nomads in ways that were inhumane and cruel. His descendants violently ended Pugachev's Rebellion, which was the largest nomad fight against the injustice of the Russians. Around the same time, Elizabeth Petrovna watched as close to one million Jungars were destroyed by the Manchu regime, all within less than one year. Injustice grew both from the Chinese and the Russians. Only thanks to your family's opium idea did pressure from the East decrease.

Kenesary Kassymuly, the last khan of the Kazakhs,
could not tolerate such injustice any longer and
rebelled against the Russians. He wanted to unite
the Kazakhs, Uzbeks, Bashkirs, Kyrgyz people, and
what remained of Jungars to continue our nomadic
way of life. He was betrayed by a Kyrgyz manap and
beheaded. His head was sent to the Russians as a
token of loyalty.

The head has still not been returned to our country
and it is likely not to exist anymore. In fact, now that
I am reading more of European history, I am realizing
the whole story may have been a cynical joke played
on the sensibilities and pride of my people. After all,
Germany played this sort of a trick with the skull of
Chief Mkwawa. In fact, the British government came
up with the idea of including the clause that mentions
the Tanzanian chief's skull in the Versailles Treaty.
Bravo! The Tanzanians did end up fighting on your
side after you returned them what could have indeed
been the chief's head.

My "adopted" father, Professor Ansar Tolengitovich,
did not want to rely on a skull legend. He wanted to
bring back a sample of royal greatness to the Kazakhs.
That's why I was cloned from the remains of Kenesary.
I am not alone in this country. A reincarnation of
Amursana, the last prince of the Jungars, is also in the
area. He is my uncle.

It was too late when the Romanov and Aisin Goro
families realized they committed grave sins against
nomads who had always been supportive and friendly.
We were natural inhabitants of the Eurasian steppe,
and we domesticated horses, invented the chariot, and

connected sedentary civilizations with one another. The ideas and goods passed through our minds and lands. We made sure that ethical norms and codes of conduct were respected. Our words lasted longer than written contracts. So when the nomad civilizations were destroyed, both the Romanov and Aisin Goro families were corrupted by insane ideologies and eliminated by their followers. Communism was quickly followed by fascism.

Now, however, I have returned as the rightful descendant of Genghis Khan, and I am still young. Uncle Amursana, who promised to come back on a white horse, your favorite animal, is indeed reincarnated in the body of Abdullah the Uyghur. Amursana is ready to lead the Mongols of the East and of the West. I am ready to lead the Kazakhs and any other Turks who want to follow us.

Your Majesty, all we need is your permission. Restore us our noble titles and help bring back nomadic civilization. I am sure you understand my situation better than anyone else in this world. You know what I mean. I have the honor of being Your Majesty's humble and obedient servant.

Sincerely,
Kenesary the Second

CHAPTER 10

JACK IN THE BOX

—

2036, *London, England*

British bureaucracy worked as efficiently in the modern era as it ever had in the times of their imperial glory. Her Majesty replied within fourteen days and invited both Kenesary and Amursana for an afternoon tea at 4:00 p.m. It turned out, however, that the two nomads were not the only ones invited. By either court protocol or some accident, His Excellency Eldar Jose, the Ambassador of Kazakhstan to the United Kingdom, was invited as well. Representing the Administration of President Qozganov, who had finally won his election in Kazakhstan, Ambassador Jose did the best he could to know about everything that had to do with his country. His loyalty to the Qozganov regime was unquestionable.

Eldar Jose was born in the United States. His mother, Ulbolsyn, a native of the southern Kazakh city of Shymkent, had decided to stay in Los Angeles after her "work and travel" trip. Although she still had only one year left to graduate from Akhmet Yassawi University and although her parents had long been half-joking about marrying her off to the son of the deputy chief of the Shymkent police, she fell in love with Marina del Ray and Mulholland Drive.

Moreover, as her mother's excessively Southern sister in Shymkent had rightly suspected, the two streets were not the only avenues of love; a Mexican had to be involved as well. Juan Carlos Jose, who hailed from the city of Guadalajara, was indeed involved in this matter. His way to the neighboring United States, however, had been much more difficult than what Ulbolsyn had gone through. But it was worth it, for he met the beauty from Shymkent.

Juan Carlos and Ulbolsyn met at Jack-in-the-Box near Staples Stadium, where they worked together on the night shift. At first, Juan Carlos assumed Ulbolsyn was just another Asian exchange student, quiet and overly focused on work. But it turned out that Ulbolsyn would never shut up, teaching Juan Carlos some random Kazakh words he could not refuse to learn out of his politeness and growing respect for the girl.

The true test of his chivalry, however, came one night when the Kazakh boxing champion "Triple G" lost his titles to Canelo the Mexican. Some drunk Latinos celebrating the victory dressed up in costumes of a fake Kazakh journalist and started harassing people with beautiful turquoise flags. Jack-in-the-Box staff Kazakhs were not an exception. Juan Carlos, of course, stood up for the girl and chased away the intruders. That's when Ulbolsyn realized Juan Carlos deserved another kind of attention.

After Eldar was born, however, Juan Carlos's parents in Guadalajara got sick. He left to see them, telling Ulbolsyn he would never forgive himself if he did not go to support them. Unfortunately, he never came back, largely thanks to the New Wall. After some time, it no longer made sense for Ulbolsyn to live in the Mexican community. Local women did not like that she lived alone, and it became more apparent that she was being excluded from social and cultural activities. No one invited her to make tamales before holidays, for example.

She did not want Eldar to grow up a pariah and one day decided to move to New York City, where she settled at Sheepshead Bay in Brooklyn, close to the Russian Brighton Beach, and found a job at the Kazakh consulate in Manhattan. The job came with perks, as Eldar got a chance to attend language lessons and meet high-level officials from an early age. As a result, Eldar learned a lot of tricks and strategy from Kazakh diplomats and treated them with the respect meant for Juan Carlos.

During the pandemic, Ulbolsyn's parents got sick with no one in the city to look after them. Even though they had named their daughter Ulbolsyn ("Let there be a son!"), no son had been born following her birth. As the oldest daughter, she therefore had to take the responsibilities of the son. The consulate had no work to do, as very few people in Kazakhstan could come to the United States at that time due to travel restrictions. That's why she decided to go back to Shymkent and live with her parents.

In some ways, she could see that living among relatives could help Eldar become stronger and healthier although she did not want him to miss out on educational opportunities that Brooklyn had to offer. What she did not know was that Shymkent had set up two Nazarbayev Intellectual Schools that offered the British curriculum, and Eldar, with his diplomatic Kazakh and Brooklyn English, would pass the admission exams with flair.

Nazarbayev University in Nur-Sultan followed Nazarbayev Intellectual School. Eldar Jose excelled in academics and salsa dancing. Ulbolsyn could see how Eldar was becoming more like Juan Carlos in dynamic and chaotic Kazakhstan. It was as if the concrete jungles of Brooklyn had prevented Eldar's full transformation into the energetic and ambitious boy she had wanted him to be. Yet she also noticed how he was forgetting his democratic upbringing and becoming more like her Communist father: speaking what the Government wanted to hear, flattering the leaders, and always using the proletarian we: "the people and I." In many ways, this attitude helped him get promoted, first in his extracurricular activities, then in student government, and eventually in real government. He volunteered for the Qozganov Election Team and passionately wanted the fallen hero to win in the upcoming elections.

Qozganov did indeed win. The volunteers became the new president's strong supporters, helping him with everything. At first, Eldar brought his boss the best cigars he could find in Nur-Sultan. He went so far as to order some from South America and Cuba. Then Eldar started bringing Qozganov high-quality alcoholic drinks, including his favorite brand of mezcal. Perhaps impressed by the floating worm, the president grew to like Eldar so much he invited the young man to his weekly saunas. This was not an especially rare event, but not everyone made it further than going to saunas with the boss. So when Eldar learned that Qozganov had invited him for a hunting trip, he was elated. Taking someone with a gun to the wild steppe meant a lot.

On that trip and through this and that, Qozganov learned he could trust this ambitious half-Mexican young man. Eldar's career was secure, and in a short while he was appointed to the Embassy in the United Kingdom, where he worked on the most important projects, such as the Opposition, the Miners, and "the Royals." The Miners referred to Britcoin, which controlled bitcoin mining in Russia and Kazakhstan. These powerful people could help protect the foreign assets of the Kazakh elite and could intervene when media outlets became overly outrageous.

"The Royals," of course, referred to Kenesary and Amursana, whose rebellious nature was known to both the Russians and the Chinese. Apparently, Mels had bragged somewhere that he helped clone Kenesary after the young man left Kazakhstan. The secret service had asked the ambassador to keep them under control, just in case. That's how Eldar Jose ended up with Kenesary and Amursana at the Royal Court, sipping his afternoon tea elegantly and professionally, much like his "uncles" did at the Kazakh Consulate in New York City.

Kenesary and Amursana felt like entrepreneurs about to pitch their startup idea to Sand Hill Road venture capitalists in the Silicon Valley. They were worried and knew no other clone or avatar might enjoy such a historical opportunity ever again. Even though the queen granted knighthoods quite often, she rarely created new monarchs. It was one thing to bless an Oxbridge alum commoner as a ruler in India or Pakistan, but it was an entirely different matter to bring the unpredictable descendants of Genghis Khan back into the game.

With the Manchus and Mongols long gone, it had been comfortable to share the world with the Japanese Emperor, the Son of Heaven in the Land of the Rising Sun. He was far away, and his country was technologically advanced. But the young gentlemen she was going to drink tea with came from the middle of nowhere, and it was not clear whether they would help Her Majesty's mining activities in Kazakhstan or not. She did not want some nomad romantics to undermine her aggressive bitcoin accumulation strategy. Yet, it was important to see them because, like it or not, they had the blood, and she knew only too well that the blood had a tendency to surface when opportunity appeared. She did not want to be startled by some unpleasant surprise.

The gentlemen turned out to be quite pleasant. Kenesary overcame his arrogance and employed his Attila accent instead of his usual Russian one. His pre-nuke genes and carefully selected clothes made him look tall and regal. Amursana acted more like a hospitable Uyghur restauranteur than a reincarnate Jungar prince. Even though the queen insisted on pouring her tea herself, he grabbed the teapot with the speed and elegance of a tightrope-walker. He was impressed by how young she looked. He pulled in his stomach slightly not to appear as fat as he actually was. Still, despite their claims and backgrounds, Eldar Jose looked much more "presentable," as it was common to say in diplomatic circles, and behaved impeccably.

"Thank you for this opportunity to be in your presence, Your Majesty. It is a great pleasure to meet you!" said Eldar, taking control of the conversation.

"The pleasure is entirely mine," replied the queen, looking at Eldar and sensing his common origin. She could feel that he was trying too hard and pushing like a torpedo. No descendant of Genghis Khan would have done that.

"We are here to introduce ourselves and inquire about your mood and health, Your Majesty," began Kenesary.

"How nice of you, young man. I am curious as to what your name means," wondered the queen.

"It means Yellow Bug. Kazakhs have a custom of naming their children unpleasant names to avoid jealousy and the evil eye. Alas, it did not save my predecessor."

Kenesary felt slightly sad as he responded. Part of the reason was the luxurious and comfortable atmosphere of the queen's palace. He sighed as he realized the difference between her and him. His residence was a small dorm room with a broken chiffonier. He did not even own a tiny piece of land, not even in Kazakhstan, the ninth largest country in the world. He and Tomyris still lived in Ansar Tolengitovich's old apartment, an "aerial yurt."

"What a wise custom! And what does your name mean?" she asked Amursana.

"My name means Clear Mind, Your Majesty," responded Amursana dutifully.

Eldar thought it was ironic that a brainwashed man decided to name himself Clear Mind. He was about to mentally record this interesting idea to share his witticism with a fellow diplomat, but the queen then inquired about his name as well.

"My name comes from Arabic. It means Peace," replied Eldar in a soothing voice.

"How wonderful, and I know what *Jose* means," answered the queen. "I am glad you are all here today. I started reading *The Secret History of the Mongols* in anticipation of our meeting. It is an amazing document, recently translated again at Cambridge. I highlighted a couple of paragraphs there. One quote I liked from Genghis Khan is this:

'With one of my descendants governing, you cannot go wrong if you observe my decree and refrain from changing it. Even if Ögödei's descendants were born such that they would not be eaten by a cow though wrapped in sedge, or eaten by a dog though wrapped in fat, surely one of my descendants will be born good?'

I understand Genghis Khan wanted Ögödei's descendants to be recognized as great khans. You, Kenesary, are a descendant of Jochi, who may not have actually been Genghis Khan's son. And still, you want me to recognize you as Khan?"

"The document is called *Secret History* for a reason," responded Kenesary, his words bordering on aggression before he quickly realized this was not the right way to go. "However, I do not want to be recognized as the Great Khan, Your Majesty. I only want to regain my title as the Khan of the Kazakhs. My friend, Amursana, wants to be recognized as the Prince of Jungars. Surely, having been completely destroyed as a nation, almost obliterated from the face of the Earth, Jungars would respect you for bringing back their last prince. Their veneration may not go as far as that of the tribe in Vanuatu who still treat the late Prince Philip as their god, but you never know." Kenesary was suddenly afraid the queen might notice the traces of sarcasm in this last response, but the queen became enthusiastic and nostalgic at the same time.

"Indeed. It would be an act of historic justice to this unfortunate nation. Besides, it helps that Amursana also happens to be in the body of an Uyghur. They too have suffered culturally lately. So perhaps we could indeed shoot two hares with one bullet," replied the queen, much to Eldar's dismay.

"We are a democratic and secular country, Your Majesty," replied Eldar, displaying his protest. He would get demoted if Kenesary and Amursana were to receive their titles.

"So is the United Kingdom, your excellency." The queen did not like Eldar, and "we are a democracy, and royal families can do whatever they want here" did not have to be spoken for the words to hand in the air. Even if it had not been recommended by her advisors, she still wanted to help the young gentlemen immediately. Kenesary and Amursana felt regal.

CHAPTER 11

BACK IN EURASIA

2036, Nur-Sultan, Kazakhstan

When President Qozganov learned about the queen's recognition of Kenesary and Amursana's claims to royalty, he could feel a burning sensation in the pit of his stomach. It was unbelievable how much applying double-standards was such a normal practice for Westerners.

"They could be mining your bitcoin with one hand and undermining your throne with the other," murmured the president, as if talking to his special self.

Eldar Jose decided not to respond to that unique outburst of political anger. He could see the president's hologram getting extremely irritated in the Ambassador's study room. The apparition's gaze darted around; it clearly wanted to pick up Eldar's books and throw them onto the floor, and it only got angrier because it could not really do that, of course. To satisfy the old man's desire, Eldar moved to tip a couple of the less valuable books off the bookshelf, but he did so rather gently. This infuriated Qozganov even more.

"You never finish any matter that comes to your hands! You start, you imitate a stormy activity, but you never really finish it! That's your problem, *amigo.*"

Again, the president brought up Eldar's Mexican heritage in a derogatory fashion. It was impossible to work with these Kazakhs. Even if one were a pure Kazakh, they would still find fault in one's tribal origin. If all were of the same tribe, they would turn to the mother's tribal lineage to find fault. If that analysis did not bear fruit, they would bring up the city of origin as an issue. The fact that Eldar's mother was from Shymkent, for example, often served as a perfectly reasonable explanation for why Eldar was so sly.

Yet better to be from any city at all than a rural village, they would keep making fun of that fact for ages. It was extremely difficult for Eldar to take this kind of culture in stride, even though he knew in reality they did not actually care. No one truly cared about all these things as much as they pretended. Very few people were extremely serious about one's nationality or tribal origin in Kazakhstan. The country prided itself in its natural adoption of pluralist and multicultural values. Tribe-talk was all small talk. People only pretended these things mattered to seem more authentic, more Kazakh. It was a way of connecting to the past in an environment where history had stopped mattering and was a political tool.

Qozganov loved Kazakhstan. He respected his predecessors. He thought all the previous presidents had accomplished a lot playing geopolitical games with the Russians, Chinese, Americans, Europeans, Turks, Arabs, and Persians. Those geopolitical games often confused the citizens; they did not know exactly who they were supposed to love and respect. Nor did they not know who a true friend was. Just in case, therefore, they loved and respected America. They even pronounced "America" as they used to pronounce "Mysyr" (Egypt) back in the ages. America, for Kazakhs, was a new Egypt—a place where a nomad could start off as a Mamluk and eventually become a Sultan. One old proverb, probably a piece of propaganda material, asserted that "it was better to be an *ultan* (shoe insole) at home than to be a *sultan* abroad." However, a lot of Kazakhs begged to disagree.

Qozganov regretted that he had underestimated Kenesary the Clone. He had thought the whole matter was some sort of a joke, the fiction of a delusional librarian from the *baraholka*. He should have listened to Mels, who had told Qozganov about the project long ago and was ready to give away any and all the details as long as he was not tortured. He did, however, insist on receiving a bottle of Jack Daniels, convinced as he was that his information was really of geopolitical importance. It was a rare Shakespearean trade with minor post-Soviet adjustments—half a kingdom for a bottle!

Back then, Qozganov was editor-in-chief of *Kazakh Pravda*, a newspaper that would not have sold a single copy had it not been contracted by the government to manufacture and deliver the truth. He had personally handled interviews when truth demanded the agreement of certain otherwise-noncooperative people although getting some useful information from the tortured proved difficult when it was clear from their looks that they were ordinary citizens with nothing in mind but survival. Qozganov's ignorance may have helped Kenesary escape the unnecessary monitoring that had been established back in the early years of the twentieth century to prevent children and relatives of purged and repressed elements of Soviet society from taking their revenge on the Communist government. Kazakh people knew all too well about concentration camps; they bore witness to all the terrible things that happened there as prisoners, neighbors or, worse, employees.

Now that the Kenesary issue had emerged, Qozganov did not know how to proceed. The Genechain, an AI machine that processed DNA of all living humans real time, detected some clones with no immediate living parental genotypes. Kenesary was one of the abnormalities with a clear *töre* Y-chromosome haplogroup. Kazakhstan was officially still trying to bring back Kenesary's head from Russia. Trying to destroy a new khan would be a political disaster since it was only a matter of days before Kenesary could emerge as a national celebrity, proclaiming his royal title and with the protection of the queen.

Ignoring him was not an option either. Kazakhs revered their history, and they owed the existence of their state to Genghis Khan and his descendants. Kazakhs were ready to follow anyone who claimed to be a legitimate heir to Kenesary. In this case, the new royalty was holding all the cards, since he called himself Kenesary the Second and could prove that he was genetically identical to the original Khan. The only solution, therefore, was to have the Russians deal with Kenesary the Second again. *If they succeeded with the original, they would surely succeed with the clone*, thought Qozganov. It did not even cross his mind that he was committing an act of grave treason.

* * *

Moscow's Lubyanka had been home to the KGB, FSB, and then NSB for more than a century. Yet even though it hosted the headquarters of two of the scariest organizations in the world, Lubyanka was, ironically, a place full of joy. It attracted the younger residents of Moscow to come out in droves along with the summer sun, proving especially popular with those who wanted to roller skate and stunt ride. Ever since BMX freestyle park became an Olympic event in 2020, the Russian government had set up its own BMX bike production plant to supply every teenager with a bicycle. The Eternal Head came up with the idea of incorporating BMX bikes as an essential physical education equipment in schools. It had grown disillusioned with equestrian sports and aikido, useless as they were in preparing humans for cyborg warfare.

Cybersports, roller skating, and stunt riding seemed to offer better potential. As a former security official, one anonymous representative of the Eternal Head expressed a wish in a traditional New Year's Eve speech that every citizen wearing shoulder straps, every citizen who considered themselves a defender of the Motherland, should ride a BMX. This measure led to a significant decrease in Moscow traffic, which had been hitherto impossible even with the introduction of locally made autonomous vehicles.

Ivan Andreyevich, despite his forty years of age, had to ride his BMX to Lubyanka as well. He hated the idea but convinced himself through meditation and hypnosis that his boss could not be wrong. For someone like Ivan in particular, who had been born in the now technically foreign city of Tashkent in Uzbekistan, reaching his level in the highly competitive NSB required more than being able to hold two contradictory opinions at the same time. One must also be able to expunge the ideas that the Eternal Head did not like. The trick was to detect what it *actually* liked.

Ivan Andreyevich happened to be trained for decades in figuring out people's subconscious desires at both the individual and collective levels. He, after all, had detected that most Americans *actually* and *sincerely* wanted one of their controversial leaders back in 2024. Ivan had been named a hero in a clandestine *dacha* ceremony for making it happen and helping Russia become great again. Now, however, he was assigned the less prestigious task of dealing with some Central Asian impostors.

Ivan knew from Russian history that dealing with impostors was always a dangerous affair. Successful impostors posed danger to the legitimacy of rule of the Eternal Head, who was itself afraid of the descendants of the Romanovs and of Genghis Khan due to their annoying tendency to stick to thrones for centuries. Rulers with non-dynastic nicknames, such as Lenin and Stalin, ruled for a few decades at most and did not have eternal claims to their thrones. Yet the risk was always present that if impostors were legitimized even once, they could stick around for far too long, especially if they were Central Asian. His duty was clear although Ivan found the idea of dealing with Central Asians mildly distasteful.

As someone who grew up with Kazakhs and Uzbeks, he always wanted to avoid eliminating them if at all possible. This was his way of keeping his childhood memories intact and beautiful. In his color-coded categories, his childhood was a green period. It was the only reservoir of happiness remaining in his stressful red period. To accomplish this new Central Asian mission, he had to get back to his mastery of Turkic languages and catch up with the latest writings on and from the region. Eliminating Kenesary and Amursana, tightrope walkers though they may be, seemed hardly worth the effort.

CHAPTER 12

NOUVEAU NOMADS

—

2037, Berkshire, England

Meanwhile, Kenesary and Amursana were happily enjoying their new titles in Berkshire. Having royal prefixes added to their long and unpronounceable names made the gentlemen feel more comfortable. Declaring in all seriousness that they were princes felt outrageously uplifting. *Literally*, as the older people liked to say in America. Amursana, for example, was finally allotted a small piece of land for ninety-nine years from his city council. Even though it was not a freehold ownership, the Buddhist prince figured owning the land while he was alive would be sufficient. He did not need to own this exact land in his next life.

As for Kenesary, he stopped getting papers with tear marks from his teachers at Attila. They finally started reading his essays and considering them in a new light, as pieces of work written by a person who had been blessed to talk to the queen. Most importantly, Kenesary was chosen to join Hop (Attila Society), a select group of students who acted as school prefects. As a Hopper, Kenesary could monitor students in chapel, sign them into events, and boss them around while wearing a uniform of his own design. He decided to stick a Kazakh Khanate flag on his waistcoat. His political life had started unexpectedly fast.

The new nomads decided to keep their official titles secret because it was not clear to either of them what exactly they intended to do. On the one hand, they could keep living in the West and enjoying the privileges that came with royal titles, such as invitations to special dinners, discounts at night clubs, and preferential admissions for any family members to universities of their choice. They could also talk with some assumed credibility about the histories and cultures of their respective nations at important seminars and webinars. Museums, for example, would be happy to host them while displaying some archeological findings from the steppes. But Kenesary did not like these ideas... It all seemed too boring for his adventurous spirit. As much as Amursana tried to persuade him to build a long-term plan with a view of settling on the queen's Island, Kenesary refused to consider such a un-nomadic and sedentary life.

Having kept up with political news from Central Asia, reinforced by reading up on the history of the region from dusty old books at Attila, Kenesary pictured instead a life full of adventures in Kazakhstan. With every step, he could hear the call of the steppe. Generation Q was at its prime, breaking and changing the rules of the game and challenging every status quo under the blue sky. They were bringing technological and cultural innovations to the region and transforming the way Kazakhs lived. Finally, some people were rich enough to live a nomadic life of their own design in the country, spending winters in the south and enjoying summer breeze in the north.

The new nomads all over the world found their dynamic lifestyles fulfilling and healthy. People got closer to nature and modern yurts became even more comfortable and sustainable. Every Kazakh couple could now afford an organic home. They did not have to sign up for a lifetime of mortgages and spend their lives in misery serving government officials who enriched themselves through corruption. Kenesary imagined a happy nation on the steppe and he wanted to help it leap into the future. Of course, he wanted Amursana to help him find new meaning in this social transformation.

Amursana, on the other hand, did not really want to go to Kazakhstan. Yes, Kenesary was his relative. Yes, many Uyghurs were in the country, so there would be no problem with his favorite cuisine. The problem was that Kazakhs considered Jungars to be their archenemies. Yes, if you pressed him on it, Amursana would agree that Jungars nowadays were simply convenient enemies for Kazakhs, because most of the Jungars had been destroyed by Qianlong's armies in the 1750s. As Eldar Jose knew too well, Kazakhs seemed to enjoy a dead enemy to solidify their unity, because declaring the Russians or Chinese as enemies could be devastating politically. Kazakhs were not as passionate about historical memory as others; they needed to be pragmatic.

Unfortunately, if our Kazakh-Mexican diplomat and reincarnated Jungar prince shared one trait, it was the inability to not take such things personally. Amursana had no desire to be considered an enemy of any type in a country where being of a wrong tribe at a party was risky enough, not to mention being a Jungar soul in an Uyghur body. Yet, for all that, he did not want Kenesary to be alone. Having gone through the internship program in Xinjiang, Amursana knew what it meant to mess with totalitarian regimes.

Reminding himself further of Abylai Khan's kindness toward Amursana in the 1750s, the reincarnated Amursana decided to return a favor by helping the great Khan's grandson. It was time to start putting Leila's lessons to practice and meditate on this idea. Through these transcendental techniques, Amursana wanted to observe Abylai Khan back in the Burabay of the 1750s and figure out what he was thinking while hosting the first Amursana.

I would much rather face a sharp Jungar spear than a piercing word of a Kazakh. And aitys has a lot of the latter. As a child, I used to love attending these poetry battles, especially aitys rounds during Nauryz. But as I suddenly converted from being a spectator to a subject, my affection became inanimate too.

However, I had to be present in this aitys. And I had to go there enthusiastically. In fact, I sponsored this battle of poets a year before out of a sale of ten thousand military horses to the Manchus. Things seemed beautiful then. It appeared that one of my better plans could finally work out. But one thing life teaches us is that we are nothing but tumbleweed on the steppe.

Funny... I too used to like poetry as a child. My very first poem was about a tumbleweed. I managed to relate it to the fate of my people, who were moving behind their horses wherever there were no Jungars, whose men had been our enemies and whose women—our favorite wives.

The aitys went well, nevertheless. I focused on the style and creativity of the poets rather than on the subject matter. My skin has gotten thicker when it comes to criticism. Perhaps that shows I am getting more experienced. Of course, some of the poets supported me by criticizing my wives and sons more than my policies. Fortunately, they lost; I would otherwise be criticized for interfering with the judges.

It is not for a lack of words that poets lose in these battles but for the lack of logical consistency. Once the argument weakens, the crowd feels it and it is hard to maintain an unjust position through beautiful words alone. It was quite revealing to hear what the poets had to say about Amursana, my Jungar friend, who is now a political refugee and is staying in Burabay under my protection. Most of my people are against our support for him, but what do commoners understand about geopolitics, noble blood, and friendship? Poets, particularly, are happy to forgo reason for a rhyme. What a bad trade indeed. The Kerei poet, for example, said:

Finally the day has come to our lands,
When not only the night equals the day,
But also poets equal the chamberlains,
And may speak their minds, dare I say.
Can a wolf of yesterday become a loyal dog?
Can a beaten fox befriend a noble eagle?
Whenever wolves come, dragons follow,
Filling yurts with tears and sorrow.

There is a saying among Kazakhs that "you should not mention you are a poet in the land of Atygai" for you will quickly be put to shame by their talent. But the Kerei continued his line very well and the Atygai poet could not respond properly. His emphasis on making a joke and showing that we are strong did not resonate with the public, who would normally shout out support for him. So, I was standing there and thinking how to help my friend, Amursana. My guest, my son-in-law, needed my support more than I needed his when I was their esteemed prisoner...

Amursana enjoyed these new meditations on his past life. Not only did his reincarnated soul remember everything about himself after the queen's recognition, but it also learned to read other people's minds from his past. The past was getting more obvious.

Kenesary loved it when Amursana would sit cross-legged and begin to meditate, speaking in tongues along the way. His perfect soft Uyghur and superficial coarse Mongolian language skills combined well to produce Kazakh sounds. Kenesary would shiver each time he heard his grandfather Abylai's voice coming from Amursana's meditation sessions. As soon as the sessions were over, Kenesary would ask for more. Sometimes Amursana would oblige, at times repeating utterings from his previous meditations. Whether he knew it or not, Amursana often repeated the following words of Abylai.

Kazakh-Jungar relationships have always been ambiguous. We called them Jungar and Oirat when we wanted to emphasize our enmity and we called them Kalmak when we wanted to point out that our roots were the same. When we were blessed with knowledge and inspiration from Allah centuries ago, Jungars decided to stay loyal to their shamanic practices. So we started calling them Kalmaks, which means the ones who decided to stay, in this particular case, in disbelief, or in Jahilia, as our imams like to point out. But they did not stay in disbelief for long and soon accepted Buddhism, the yellow faith of the Tibetan variety. It was quite amusing for Kazakhs to see some Jungars completely bald and ascetic. Finally, our ancestors joked, there will not be much competition for your ladies.

Jungars, however, once again proved that pacifism does not work on the steppe. The battle for survival becomes more important than meditation. Jungars have been attacking us for the last hundred years and I was taken as an amanat (collateral) in order to prevent more fights. Thank god that my ancestor Genghis Khan introduced this system of taking collaterals. He made unnecessary destruction and killing illegal in his Yassa laws. So Galdan Tseren had no other option but to take me as his guest and captive at the same time. In his camp I met Amursana. He was a student who had just returned from Khanbaliq (Beijing) and he liked spending time with his grandfather, from whom he could learn real lessons and wisdom from the steppe. I too enjoyed talking to Galdan Tseren and those were great times in "prison." I learned to speak the languages of Jungars and Manchus, and it was fascinating to learn their ways of writing from Amursana. Not that he was a particularly good teacher when drunk.

Little did I know back then that this Amursana would one day come to me to seek refuge from the very emperor he respected so much and studied with in Khanbaliq. The problem with Qianlong was that he cared too much what the common Chinese thought of him. Too involved in matters of the court, he was forgetting his Manchu nomad traditions. That's why he decided to go against his nomad brothers, even though he too came from the same blood as did our forefathers and the forefathers of the Mongols and Jungars. It is funny that Russians call them "Manchur" because we have a word that sounds similar, meaning a man who forgets his self and his identity. It comes from Persian and is pronounced Mankurt. How does one not become a Mankurt?

For some reason at this point Amursana would always stop. In a way, Kenesary understood that Amursana became a Mankurt at his internship program because he forgot his real identity and religion. At the same time, however, Amursana found a new identity that was brave and sly. Perhaps, Kenesary thought, that fire really matters in a man. As long as the fire is there, it does not matter what identity it takes. It was important to find that inner fire and figure out what Kenesary the First would have done had he been here and now. Would he depose Qozganov?

PART III

AI PUGACHEV

CHAPTER 13

KOSTYA THE HACKER

2015, Poltava, Ukraine

On the outskirts of the relatively old city of Poltava in Ukraine, Kostya practiced coding in his grandmother's *dacha*. A proud descendant of the Cossacks that had supported Yemelyan Pugachev in his uprising of the nomads against the Russian Empress in the eighteenth century, Kostya was not emotionally suited to work for the government and hated any kind of routine tasks. He grew up with other Cossack boys in a tough neighborhood called Kobyschany, which had seen its better days.

In addition to boxing, which Ukrainian boys loved so much, Kostya also grew interested in coding from an early age. His grandmother's *dacha* served as a gathering place for a group of emigre Russian hackers who had refused to work for the FSB, Russia's successor to the KGB, and therefore operated out of Poltava. Kostya's grandmother had been a primary school teacher of one of the hackers, and she enjoyed their absolute trust. As a token of gratitude for her constant supply of goat milk and *pirozhki*, the team took Kostya on as an apprentice and taught him how to think, code, and hack.

Looking at it from the outside, few would imagine that such a dilapidated *dacha* could be home to some of the most brilliant hackers of Russia's new generation. While their college friends were enjoying what the Silicon Valley had to offer in Northern California, these knights decided to spend time in Poltava, where Peter the Great had held decisive battles against the Swedes. It was ironic because now the Russian hackers were on the side of the Swedes, working with some serious Scandinavian activists and Julian Assange on a monumental Wikileaks project, as well as helping a group of Americans with their digital currency project. Poltava was also a place where nomad Scythians used to roam thousands of years ago. In a more recent history, it was a battlefield where relatives of Kazakhs had fought against Cossacks and where Cossacks had fought against relatives of Jungars. Blood was an essential component of the Poltavan soil.

Kostya quickly came to realize that his masters could easily become multimillionaires if they so willed, but they were pursuing a bigger goal. As he watched them coding and discussing, he dreamed of one day joining their ranks and influencing world events. When a representative of the Eternal Head ordered a group of Cossacks to beat up Pussy Riot activists during the Winter Olympic Games in Sochi, Kostya got particularly angry at the violence and un-nomadic behavior shown toward these ladies, especially toward his favorite anarchist feminist warrior—Nadezhda Tolokonnikova. At that point Kostya realized the nomads needed a strong noble leader, someone who could inspire his generation to feel the essence of life once again and to stop being slaves to those who were weak and wicked in their nature. He wanted someone like Pugachev to be back.

Pugachev, after all, had accomplished something especially notable. Standing against an empire, he had managed to unite all the nomads, despite their religious and linguistic differences. The secret to Pugachev's success was simple. The risks of enslavement to an increasingly oppressive Russian Empire were too great, and it was necessary to defend the old way of living, the old way of thinking. Freedom was essential for all the nomads. Pugachev did, however, see fit to add one small trick to his elevator pitch—impersonating the supposedly dead husband of Catherine the Great, Peter III. Catherine was an alien who did not understand the locals; Peter was the only one capable of keeping the balance between East and West, between noble and commoner, between Cossack and Czar. Nadezhda Tolokonnikova would have been a greater queen than Catherine, but she was imprisoned, and the Eternal Head had gone so far as to hire a prison guard with a PhD in philosophy to make sense of her correspondence with other philosophers. Ideas—like identities—were dangerous in Russia.

The more Kostya thought about the issue, the more he became convinced that the Eternal Head had to be deposed. The Kremlin had to be dealt with and it necessitated drastic measures. Kostya, however, differed from our heroes in believing that one leader, however strong and charismatic, was useless. The rallying myth of Pugachev as Peter III, after all, had centered on him as a divine blessing rather than an instigator, came down from the halls of power to give his approval to the righteous rebels. Bringing back Pugachev would not help, and it would take too long before he grew up anyway. Kostya had a reason to be in a rush. By the time a newborn could grow up to free Nadezhda, she would be as old as the singer Pugacheva herself. She would still be attractive to young men, Kostya clarified to himself. In any case, Pugachev's ideas were what mattered. Fighting the Eternal Head required building an artificial intelligence capability on Poltavan soil. Thus began Kostya's mission, and a new artificial intelligence machine that would be called AI Pugachev. His mentors applauded his technological innovations, even if they did not know his ultimate purpose.

Brimming with nascent pan-nomadism, Kostya got interested in studying Central Asian and Mongolian history. Nadezhda had been released from prison but, rather than bow down in gratitude to the Eternal Head's mercy, he simply decided that he could now afford to play the long game. Pugachev the blessing was well on his way to being reborn, but even the saintly Peter III needed his loyal generals, and the boundless steppes seemed like the perfect place to get them. He realized the Eurasian ecosystem he wanted to create would be incomplete without Kenesary and Amursana, both of whom were unfortunate victims of Russian and Chinese aggression taken to the extreme. Politics and nature had already been playing along to help Kostya execute his plan. During his visit to Kazakhstan in 2013, China's President Xi Jinping had presented his Belt and Road Initiative at Nazarbayev University, making the news even in *Poltava*. After that, the CCP began sponsoring internship programs for millions of Uyghurs in Xinjiang right in the very place where close to a million Jungars had been destroyed in the 1750s.

At home in Poltava, Kostya would take care of AI Pugachev with so much love. He wanted his machine to be one of the most powerful entities solely dedicated to making nomads great again. AI Pugachev was fluent in more than fifty human languages and could quickly identify the myriad dialects in Turkic, Slavic, and Mongolian languages. AI Pugachev read and analyzed millions of blog posts, articles, books, documentaries, lectures, and dissertations on the history, literature, and culture of the nomads. It knew more about Kazakhs, Bashkirs, Yakuts, Cossacks, Evenks, Kalmaks, Oirats, Mongols, Manchus, Mamluks, Kyrgyz and Buryats than all the Oriental Institutes had ever known or could know.

AI Pugachev was extremely knowledgeable and ethical in nomadic and geopolitical matters. Kostya wanted it to be stronger than any American, Russian, or Chinese AI supercomputer. Because of his constant interactions with Russian hackers, he learned how to improve its capability. The most important task was to guarantee that AI Pugachev was decentralized enough and did not depend on its Poltava location alone. Growing up in Ukraine, Kostya was superstitious to such a degree that he would not be surprised if fate one day brought a plane down upon the supercomputer, or if Poltava suddenly ceased to be part of his dear country. After Ukraine had voluntarily given up its nuclear arsenal in the early 1990s, the country became weak both militarily and politically. No way would Kostya give up control of AI Pugachev, which was even more strategically important than a bunch of nuclear warheads that never got used.

With some help from AI Pugachev, Kostya was able to hack one internship program's data center, take over the smartphone control system, and brainwash someone inside to impersonate Amursana. He was lucky to find Abdullah, who was a perfectly suitable character with a history of hallucinations and demonstrated persistence in idealistic matters. Kostya would guide this impostor and prepare him to lead Siberian and Chinese nomads, all of whom were expecting him to come back for more than 250 years anyway. It was high time for a prophecy to be fulfilled.

When the Great Pandemic hit in 2020 and the time arrived for a great reset, Kostya realized it was an opportunity of a lifetime to brainwash Professor Ansar Tolengitovich in Almaty. The professor had come to his attention sometime before, thanks to his unique access to some of the most important genetic material in Central Asia. *He* could clone the last khan of the Kazakhs. AI Pugachev sent targeted information to Ansar via YouTube and other websites. It constantly bombarded the man with "random" suggestions to watch short videos from fringe pseudo-historians who were all over the internet. The goal was to convince Ansar that it was necessary to clone Kenesary—and that it was his idea. Kazakhs were already trying to return the last khan's head from the Russians, but the head would have been useless for Kostya's plan. He needed a real man, a real khan.

As Yemelyan Pugachev had done in the eighteenth century, Kostya hoped that AI Pugachev would be able to once again unite all the nomads and make sure that Russia would no longer be under sedentary domination. Peter the Great had made a great mistake by betraying his old faith and people. He moved the capital to St. Petersburg and made Moscow and Kazan, the friendly cities of the nomads, look like villages. It was necessary to bring back glory to the steppe. It was necessary to educate and free the Cossacks from Russian exploitation. Kostya felt absolutely certain that he and AI Pugachev could achieve their goals.

CHAPTER 14

WORLD NOMAD GAMES

———

2038, Burabay, Kazakhstan

People react differently to violence. Some become afraid while some become brave. After his traumatic witnessing of the Pussy Riot incident during the Winter Olympic Games in Sochi, Kostya became brave. Not only did he figure out how to help his Cossacks become more ethical and kinder, but he also decided to become an expert in all things nomadic and chivalrous. As a long-time gamer and recent hacker, he wanted to learn more about the nomads through their games. After all, aren't adults simply playing more advanced forms of their childhood preoccupations? Isn't life mostly about who plays what and with whom?

With this intention, in September 2014 Kostya decided to visit Cholpon-Ata near the world-famous Issyk-Kul in Kyrgyzstan, which was hosting the First World Nomad Games. Kostya wanted to get a feeling for what it meant to be a real nomad that he was missing in his native, overly Europeanized Poltava. Seeing strong nomads from all over Central Asia and falling in love with the emerging platform,

Kostya wished that sometime in the future he could organize a *qurultai*, or a conference, of nomadic leaders at one of those games.

Such a moment finally arrived in 2038, when grown-up Kostya asked AI Pugachev to arrange for Kenesary and Amursana to appear as important guests at the World Nomad Games in Burabay, Kazakhstan. The new nomads, having received their regal titles just recently, were delighted at the opportunity to mingle with their "subjects." For Kenesary, who'd spent most of his life in Almaty and Berkshire, the oasis of Burabay was very special and interesting because the original Kenesary was born and grew up in the area. Even Abylai Khan ruled from either Burabay or the city of Turkestan, depending on the season and political situation.

Kenesary was surprised that tourists still liked to visit the rebel khan's favorite cave, where he first kissed his beloved. The legend, however, had it that the rebel khan used to hide in the cave from the Russians. The Soviet propaganda machine was still in action, even fifty years after the fall of the USSR. No way would Kenesary, a battle machine himself, hide from anyone.

Amursana, too, was delighted to be back in Burabay. In addition to being a place where he learned much wisdom and fell in love with Abylai Khan's daughter, Burabay was a place of political refuge for him during the most turbulent times in Central Asian history. Kazakhstan, of course, was not as powerful anymore as it used to be during Abylai Khan's times, when he could protect anyone who was unjustly treated and needed safety. Ideals and values were extremely important back then.

Kostya did not want to introduce himself to the new nomads immediately. He wanted to observe them from afar and learn more about them. Up until this meeting all he knew about them was from AI Pugachev's access to their mobile phones, school and camp records, security cameras, and other people's discussions of them. He really wanted to connect with them as naturally as possible, considering that he was the man behind AI Pugachev, which helped archeologists to find Kenesary's body, convinced Ansar Tolengitovich to clone him, hacked and controlled Leila the Xinjiang AI, brainwashed Abdullah into Amursana, introduced Tomyris to Nadezhda, and convinced the queen to meet and recognize the nomad leaders.

Another reason why Kostya did not want to approach the nomad leaders immediately was because he knew Ivan Andreyevich was also visiting Burabay and observing the new nomads. It was important to look after him as well. Kostya would not be surprised if Ivan Andreyevich could potentially deploy Novichok 8.0, the newest version of a notorious Russian toxin. The new nomads' underwear and other clothes had to be protected diligently. If the toxin got into Kenesary's underwear, there would be a need to clone him again. Ivan Andreyevich, surprisingly, had no idea that AI Pugachev was fully aware of all his plans and that Kostya was around to protect the new nomads. Still, he acted carefully, pretending to be a Siberian tourist and hiding his Muscovite accent.

As has always been the case, the games began with a huge variety of national types of wrestling. Various people from the steppe and the mountains between the Pacific and the Atlantic, between the Arctic and the Indian, were gathered in Burabay. Their ways of wrestling slightly differed but all shared the same pattern—always a winner and a loser. No one wanted to be a loser. Spectators were watching Kazakh Kuresi, Kyrgyz Kurosh, Persian Pahlavani, Turkmen Goresh,

Uzbek Kurash, Azerbaijani Gyulesh, Mongol Bokh, Russian Sambo, Korean Ssireum, Japanese Sumo, and many other forms of wrestling.

Kenesary and Amursana had never seen so many wrestlers in one place. They wondered how great it must have been for their ancestors to bring these kinds of wrestlers together and create a great nomad army. Unfortunately, there was little use for human warriors anymore, considering that many countries were switching to using cyborgs, robots, and drones in warfare. Humans were too fragile and demanded high salaries and care after the wars. They were also easily susceptible to biological weapons, whereas cyborgs and robots did not care about microbes.

The final wrestling game was the great nomad wrestling. This game did not consider participants' weight categories and wrestling styles; it reminded Kostya of *Mortal Kombat*. A huge Mongol sumo champion could fight a tiny Buryat sambo champ, for example. The game had only one rule and only one winner. The rule was to throw the opponent on the ground. Whoever landed on the ground was a loser. There was no second or third place award. Kenesary found it both Machiavellian and Genghisesque that there should be only one true winner. The principle no doubt applied to political wrestles as well. If he were serious about his political ambitions and rights, he had to learn from the wrestlers how to put the opposing force on the ground. As someone a lot of people saw as coming back from under the earth, it did not matter much if he fell on the ground a few times.

Other games included horse racing, eagle hunting, horseback archery, nomadic polo, tug-of-war and, surprisingly, tightrope walking. It turned out that tightrope walking had been included a month before the start of the games, so there were few participants. Amursana was excited at the opportunity to present his skills at such an event. The head of the organizing committee found it quite prestigious that a man from the United Kingdom would participate. While Kenesary was sure Amursana would win, he underestimated the prince's extra weight and how it affected the former professional's walking in general, not to mention the tightrope kind of walking. As a result, Amursana ended up falling ridiculously in the beginning of the walk. Even more humiliating was that he fell down on his stomach, as if he were a sack of potatoes.

Kenesary felt sorry for him. To divert the fallen prince's attention from the mishap, Kenesary took Amursana away from the crowd, faced the magnificent Kokshe the Blue Mount and said: "Try walking me through the narrower rope of time back to Kenesary Khan, though you had no chance of meeting him, and tell me what he thought of when he looked at this, Kokshe the Blue Mount." Amursana appreciated that his nephew disregarded the fall and focused on a newly acquired talent of the uncle. He sat on the nearest stone in his lotus pose and began meditating and speaking in tongues, as if he were a nineteenth century London spiritist.

Idiot. Who the hell does he think he is? I will kick his ass. He better not mess with me again by sending those Cossacks.

Kenesary had to shake Amursana physically to stop this unusual stream of consciousness and asked, "Are you sure you were accessing Kenesary's mind?" Amursana shrugged and became silent because a seemingly-Cossack man appeared from behind Kenesary.

"Hi, gentlemen. I am sorry for interrupting. Would you mind if I introduce myself?" Kostya said.

"Hello. No problem. We are just playing some game," said Kenesary.

"We are all playing games here… My name is Kostya, a short name for Konstantin."

"Nice to meet you, Kostya. My name is Kenesary and this is my friend Uncle Amursana," Kenesary replied politely. "We are in no need of short names."

"To be honest, I know quite a lot about you. It is my honor to finally meet you. I have been dreaming of meeting the nomadic leaders since 2014, when the First World Nomad Games took place in Kyrgyzstan. After all the revolutions the Kyrgyz and Kazakh people went through, I understood the importance of true leadership for nomads. I realized that democracy does not work in these lands, because people care about the leader's sacral right to rule, not one's individual talents and virtues. I read in *The Secret History of the Mongols* that all the nomad tribes promised to Genghis Khan they would never betray his offspring and would always obey. I am thinking that maybe all our problems began from the fact that we betrayed those *white bones*…"

"What do you have to do with us, anyway? Aren't you a white Christian man?" asked Kenesary.

"Where do you think the descendants of Mamai go? I am a proud Cossack. I know. You have all the reasons to hate us for what the Russian tsars made us do to your people and especially to the people in Siberia… It is true, nevertheless, that some of us are descendants of the Mongols of the Golden Horde and of the Kipchaks before them," replied Kostya.

This was shocking for Kenesary. He never thought those bloodthirsty Cossacks could actually be related somehow to Kazakhs, Mongols, and Jungars.

"Why also do you think the nomads followed Pugachev and sacked Kazan?" asked Kostya.

"Well, certainly not because they actually thought Yemelyan was a Romanov," retorted Kenesary. They all laughed at the young scholar's sarcasm.

"I invite you to join me on a trip to Nur-Sultan, young men," said Kostya. "You are going to meet some very interesting people there."

Ivan Andreyevich had watched the avatar of the last Jungar prince attempting his tightrope walking show. He wondered if this could be a good chance to "scripple" Amursana. After their notorious poisoning attempt of a Russian family in the United Kingdom, the word Ivan came up with had stuck within the Moscow toxic unit. "Scrippling" Amursana was not as interesting, however. They could find potential use for this strange man, who was conveniently both a Jungar and a Uyghur, in Russia's dealings with China. Kenesary, though, was not a welcome guest in modern times. Any kind of independent leadership and strategic thinking had to be crushed among the Kazakhs, preferably by the Kazakhs themselves.

After the exodus and deaths from Goloshchekin's artificial hunger on the steppe and Stalin's repressions and purges, leadership traits became rare in Kazakhstan. Whenever such traits were noticed, the Communist Party was quick to find "kompromat" for such people and use them to serve the Soviet Union's interest. There were, of course, some leadership genes in remote villages and rural areas, but those people lived in such wretched conditions that they would never have a chance to exercise their talents. So went the Party logic a long time ago and so thought the Eternal Head. In addition, since those rural people mostly spoke Kazakh, had no access to proper medical service, and received substandard education due to a lack of teachers in faraway villages, city Kazakhs themselves would make sure they would never get office jobs, restricting themselves to menial work. *Funny people, those Kazakhs,* thought Ivan Andreyevich, as he was observing people around him and trying to find the new nomads.

CHAPTER 15

NUR-SULTAN CITY

———

2038, Nur-Sultan, Kazakhstan

As Kostya, Kenesary, and Amursana approached Nur-Sultan, the beautiful night of Saryarqa, or "the Yellow Backbone of the Steppe" as this region was known among the nomads, was gradually letting its stars disappear in city lights. It was fascinating to enter the city from the steppe, reminding Kostya of his trips to Nevada with Russian hackers when he was young. They would drive sports cars from Los Angeles to Las Vegas only to lose some of that crazy crypto money gambling because they had too much of it anyway. It was long before the Metaverse pulled in every connected soul and mind with its tentacles.

Much like Las Vegas, Nur-Sultan had its own Pyramid, Strat-like observation tower, new buildings of all sorts and styles, and, most importantly, ambitious people. Even though the city had changed its name many times, the culture of new people coming to the city from all over the Steppe and Siberia stayed. The city used to be called Tselinograd ("The City of Virgin Lands" in Russian) during the Soviet times, and then it regained its old name of Akmola ("The White Graveyard") before becoming Astana ("The Capital" in Kazakh), and ultimately Nur-Sultan.

Kenesary and Amursana, however, both thought of Karakorum when they saw the city. Karakorum was a ruined capital of the Mongol Empire. In some old books at Attila, Kenesary had read about the unique nomadic design of Karakorum, which featured a Silver Tree made by Italians in the center of the city. Nur-Sultan, too, had such a tree-like structure called Baiterek. The role of Karakorum was to serve as a political headquarter, as a power center where orders would emanate from the Great Khan to remote provinces of the Mongol Empire. But the city did not last long. It was only natural for Kenesary to wonder how long Nur-Sultan would last.

While the country was a chief supplier of uranium, oil, bitcoin, and gold to the rest of the world, it was not clear if the city was supplying the right decisions to the rest of the country. Everyone knew that in the past President Qozganov benefited hugely from his select army of twelve shamans, who were obsessed with divination and mass hypnosis. It was no secret that such an army existed, because the shamans were competitively selected on national TV. The shamanic army was becoming more of a useless tradition, adding no real value but ceremony. Russian nuclear reactors in Kazakhstan were guarded by hundreds of Turanian tigers and produced so much energy that the Kazakh president agreed to host one of the most powerful AI machines in the world. It was, of course, called "The Shaman." Among its many peculiarities, suffice it to say that The Shaman insisted that its pronouns be "we" and "us." Everyone knew that The Shaman, *de facto*, ruled the country.

Technically, however, the country still held elections every five years. Somehow, right before the elections, people would suddenly discover that Qozganov was an ideal president. He would find ways to liken himself to the public and make the most unexpected decisions. It was his idea, for example, to host the World Nomad Games in Burabay. With the help of The Shaman, he was able to figure out how to make the event sustainable and even bring some money to the country's budget. To further support his nomadic agenda, he claimed that by 2040 Kazakhstan would finally bring Kenesary's head back home and organize a proper burial for the last Khan of the Kazakhs in the beautiful city of Turkestan, which served as the spiritual and cultural capital of the Turco-Mongol Union. Qozganov also pointed out that the head would pass any and all necessary genetic tests and that the data would be publicly available.

* * *

Kostya knew surprisingly a lot about Nur-Sultan. Not much had happened in the city since 2017, when it hosted a specialized Expo event on Future Energy. He visited the city for the Expo and met nomads from all over Central Asia and Siberia visiting astounding Astana, as the city was called back then. Even though most of the people were dressed in their best clothes and, in general, exuded happiness and confidence, he could see how poor those people actually were. He thought of his own country, where his compatriots were living substandard lives despite the country's strategic location between the East and the West. Instead of benefiting from their geography, Ukraine was suffering from its history. That trip to Astana solidified Kostya's commitment to revitalizing nomadic culture and making the long-forgotten people of Eurasia relevant once again.

Nur-Sultan enjoyed extreme road safety. In fact, it was considered one of the safest places for pedestrians because hundreds of walking bridges were set up over the roads throughout the city. According to The Shaman, it was the most optimal use for some of the notorious Light Railway Transportation system's leftover towers. Amursana found the remaining towers a perfect training ground for tight-rope walking, which was not among the suggested uses by the machine. Finding Amursana in a good mood, Kene-sary asked him to connect with Abylai Khan again, if at all possible. Perhaps Amursana could shed some light on the eighteenth-century history. But Amursana did not like those pressured meditations; he felt as if he were a spiritual merchant of some sort. He hated the feeling, but then he became entertained by the idea of meditating on one of the towers. He quickly climbed a lonely tower near Abu Dhabi Plaza and began his meditation in a lotus pose. It took less than a minute for the Jungar prince to start speaking in tongues.

Galdan Tseren had kept me in his court for quite a long time, sharing his experience and wisdom with me. We had hundreds of intimate conversations before I left. He talked about the great people of the past, his triumph over the Man-chus, his protection of the Dalai Lama, and his vision for the future. He thought the reason why Jungars were not as united as Kazakhs was because they betrayed Genghis Khan's wish and were no longer ruled by the Great Khan's descendants. Even though the Dalai Lama did occasionally bless some Jun-gar khans with "boshugtu" titles, nomads in general did not have enough respect for Dalai Lama as they do for Genghis Khan. Any Jungar glory, therefore, was short-lived and an inter-tribal fight could break the khanate into pieces. As soon as the White Queen and the Yellow Emperor noticed the approach of such factional politics, Jungars will be finished, forecasted Galdan Tseren. He would get sad after such late-night talks over kumys. I enjoyed those silent moments...

After one such prolonged silence, Galdan Tseren asked me if I would like to unite the Jungars and the Kazakhs and serve as the Great Khan of the nomads. As a rightful descendant of Genghis Khan, I would be highly successful, he thought. In fact, there was no other choice. His Swedish advisor, Johan Gustaf Renat, analyzed the Manchu and the Russian military weapons and said it would be difficult to keep up with their innovation and development speed. Eventually, Jungars and Kazakhs would lose the arms race. It was crucial that we united and invested in developing new cannons, guns, and, most importantly, military strategies. He reminded me of a Kazakh saying, which goes, "The muscular beats one person, the brainy beats one thousand." We agreed it was important to bring more teachers from the cities and improve our mobile schools.

I was not sure if I was ready to rule both Jungars and Kazakhs. It was, to be honest, sort of boring to only be the sultan of the Middle Juz. I am thinking about bringing in more people from the Kyrgyz people of Wild Stones, from the remaining people of the Nogais, from Karakalpaks of the Black Turbans... They are all Muslim, however. It is easy for us to live together and trust each other. How does one trust a Jungar as a neighbor after all that had happened? That was my concern. It made Galdan Tseren laugh.

"How do you trust a Jungar in your bed?" he asked.

"I have their full confidence after our first nights," I joked. He knew I have a number of Jungar wives.

"You do realize I hear the rumors among the first?" he said, looking slyly at me.

"Those are not the rumors… I do want to marry Topysh, your favorite daughter. She will be known as Topysh Sulu, or Topysh the Beautiful, and I promise our descendants will be future Khans," I said. She really was cute.

"I bless you, my son. Let this be the beginning of our union. But do not tell anyone of our conversation. We first need other leaders of Jungar tribes to support you. Start with befriending Amursana. He is the son of my daughter, but he is very ambitious, and he has friends in Khanbaliq."

That's how the trio learned some history. Kostya was completely impressed by this ancient way of transcending reality. Having spent too much time in the Metaverse, he felt like a tourist visiting an enchanted land of people who still saw dreams and had visions. People did not need virtual reality headsets to access the other world, and the past was strongly intertwined with the present in the steppe. Somehow, it was easier for Kenesary to trust Amursana because of the meditative sessions. Even if he was coming up with the stories and not actually receiving them from the Universe, his intentions appeared to be good. He did care for the nomads, unlike Ivan Andreyevich, who was standing behind the tower and recording what Amursana had to say.

CHAPTER 16

IVAN OF SALISBURY

———

2038, Ilyinka, Kazakhstan

Ivan was an unusual presence in Nur-Sultan, even though he resided in a sparsely populated town of Ilyinka close to the capital. Such high-ranked professional National Security Bureau officers usually visited hostile territories in Western Europe, not friendly cities in Central Asia. It was an easy mission. Ivan kept himself busy and entertained by watching people, registering new faces, and detecting various accents. He loved it when Asian people spoke Russian. It made him feel proud of his mother tongue and justified his life's work. He was, after all, hunting down the enemies of his Russian World, *russkiy mir*, that needed protection of strong men like him.

Unfortunately, most Russians had left the city when it was renamed from Tselinograd ("The City of Virgin Lands") to Akmola. It was as if they realized that there were no more virgin lands to sow, which was the main reason why the second wave of Communist missionaries relocated to Kazakhstan after World War II. When the city was renamed from Astana to Nur-Sultan, in honor of the president Nazarbayev, even the most patient Russians swapped their turquoise passports for dark red ones. Still, even with so few pale people around, Kazakhs were making abundant use of the Slavic language, as if their own Turkic was not suited to describe what was happening in ever-crazy Nur-Sultan.

Based on the conversations of the trio, Ivan realized that Amursana had serious mental issues and was a victim of some high-level brainwashing. He felt pity for the Uyghur and was glad he had decided not to kill him. The National Security Bureau Ethics Code was quite clear about such cases: *"Agents can eliminate the enemies or drive them insane; if the enemies are already insane, their insanity should be exploited."* It was a lot easier to work with insane people. Even during Soviet times, the KGB used to require its future operatives to spend months pretending to be insane in random locations throughout the USSR. Such internships required much preparation that came with a luxury of free thinking and uncensored speech.

For the first time Ivan could size up Kenesary from proximity, and clearly the rebel clone was too young; his body still had room to grow. Ivan sympathized with the clone, who came off as an idealistic teenager with no idea what he was getting into and why. Psychologists based in Moscow informed Ivan that Kenesary was essentially harmless. The khan had very basic physical training and was not good at shooting. His only danger was his genetic makeup. The fact that the khan had a tendency to make spontaneous decisions was absolutely normal for former nomads and the psychologists asked Ivan to bear with such unpredictability.

One riddle that Ivan could not figure out was Kostya. What was this Ukrainian doing in Kazakhstan and why he was hanging out with the two nomads? Ivan did not like Ukrainians after what had happened between these formerly brother nations. He was very sensitive about his language and the brave country's decision to abandon his Russian world and to stop speaking his language, imbibed though it may be with wisdom, upset the operative very much. Each time he saw Ukrainians speaking their own language made him want to throw up. He felt disgusted and offended for his mother tongue. The presence of Kostya made Ivan even more wary of the nomads and he decided to follow them wherever the trio went.

Kostya was perfectly aware of Ivan Andreyevich. AI Pugachev had checked backgrounds of every person who arrived in Nur-Sultan over the last ten years and also of people who approached Kenesary or Amursana within ten miles and had identified Ivan Andreyevich among potentially harmful elements. AI Pugachev had then checked all street camera images from the last thirty years and spotted some unusual patterns. Noticing that Ivan Andreyevich had in the past been to Salisbury in the UK as a tourist and then to the Czech Republic, Kostya ordered AI Pugachev to have his details sent to Western intelligence operatives in Nur-Sultan. In order to get their attention on him, AI Pugachev labeled Ivan Andreyevich a "Russian crypto-hacker" with plans to undermine Britcoin's mining activities in Kazakhstan. No way could Ivan Andreyevich even pee without being watched if he threatened the Anglo-Saxon monetary system in any way.

The way intelligence agencies worked completely changed in the world with the advent of artificial intelligence and the Metaverse. Old Russian NSB, however, spent too long a time admitting operatives based on physical education tests that high school students had to pass. New intelligence professionals needed to know much more about physics than physical education. Shtirlitz, the Soviet intelligence hero, type of agents was no longer useful. This resulted in having too many romantic agents among older intelligence professionals, who wanted to travel the world and do something good for their country.

Luckily for Russia, the Eternal Head figured it out and started recruiting children from the moment they were conceived. It was important to protect all kinds of data about the future agents, including their embryo pictures. Future agents needed the right vaccination, education, and ideology, and the intelligence community needed to protect their images and sounds from reaching the all-hearing devices so the AI could not recognize them in the future. The risk, of course, was that *not* being on all the social media and on AI databases was highly suspicious.

Why did this baby not have a picture on Instagram in the good-old times? Why did this baby not watch Baby Shark videos on YouTube? If such digital traces were not left somewhere, very serious questions were asked about these babies. To avoid such inquiries, managed attribution, network analysis, and other intelligence techniques were used to make sure the intelligence baby would grow up to be perfectly normal. Compared to such advanced agents, of course, Ivan felt completely useless and wanted to retire as soon as possible. His face, after all, had become a meme at some point and was all over the Metaverse. Nevertheless, Ivan had one great advantage over the younger folks. He was really good at killing real people in the real world…

* * *

Still, he had no command to kill the nomads. All Ivan had to do was follow the trio. He enjoyed this unusual company. They looked naive and somewhat detached from reality. However, he did not enjoy the requirement to send updates and reports on their moves to a certain Kazakh ambassador. To make things more complicated and technical, the ambassador was in London of all places. This made Ivan go to sleep later than usual because Eldar Jose kept asking questions about the new nomads throughout his evening. *Ambitious guy*, thought Ivan.

Ivan could also feel that there was more to Eldar Jose than met the eye. He could tell that Eldar was born somewhere in the United States. His stare was not focused enough, and he kept smiling on the calls. *Why the heck are you smiling?* thought Ivan, whenever he saw Americans displaying their beautiful teeth to him. Of course, he understood they had no other way to feel safe and build trust in a country where almost anyone could be armed to their teeth. Still, Ivan could not tolerate anything American, and Eldar Jose was proving to be a real killjoy.

Yet there was no question of disobedience. Ivan prided himself in being extremely disciplined and professional. He told Eldar everything he knew about Kostya, describing every detail. Ivan's particular focus on the Ukrainian may have made the nomads' descriptions somewhat substandard. He reported on the nomads' meeting with Tomyris and Mels, two special people for Kenesary. Even though Kenesary's mother had only stayed for a couple of days in Nur-Sultan, the mother and the son had almost never separated during their time together. Tomyris looked quite affluent, wearing fashionable clothes and looking healthy. Ivan collected enough information to conclude that she was in a fruitful relationship with a younger man.

Ivan had also run a thorough background check on Mels. Despite being slightly over seventy, Mels was still working at the baraholka library. He did not have enough in his retirement account to survive in Almaty. He had been under constant surveillance because of his connection to Kenesary, and all the Dogecoins that Ansar entrusted him with were seized away. No one would have known about them had he not decided to reveal his wallet keys when he was tortured. This trait was peculiar to people of meager means. They never hesitated to give away everything just to get rid of police and red tape. Knowing the nomads had no assets to spend, Ivan concluded he had nothing to worry about.

CHAPTER 17

THE ETERNAL HEAD

———

2038, Nur-Sultan, Kazakhstan

The Eternal Head has decided to build a new city in Siberia. The Eternal Head is changing the rules for wedding celebrations in Tatarstan. The Eternal Head has come up with a strategy to increase reproduction rate in Moscow. The Eternal Head has figured out the truth about the Second World War...

The Eternal Head seemed to influence everything in Eurasia. It was all over the news and rumors, yet no one knew much about it. People did not know what and where it was. They got accustomed to living with it and they had to trust its wisdom. It was incredible how powerful something could be given it was not seen. Some bloggers doubted its existence at all and claimed that the Eternal Head was nothing but a collective will that had been carefully filtered and analyzed. Whatever decisions it was making were based on millions of daily surveys and petitions that people so eagerly and thoughtlessly filled out. Any mistake of the Eternal Head, therefore, was in fact that of the people. Such bloggers tended to become invisible as well.

AI Pugachev was constantly bombarded by Kostya's queries about the Eternal Head. Over the years, the Poltava machine had gathered a lot of information from Russia, China, and Central Asia about the Eternal Head. AI Pugachev automatically processed all the information and shared regular reports of its investigation with Kostya. Sometimes it would take months, or even years, to process the data that kept growing in both quantity and quality.

Because AI Pugachev was programmed to share only credible knowledge pieces, statistical verification of data on the Eternal Head took more time as well. Nevertheless, Kostya was already guessing what they were dealing with, especially in light of the most recent report on the Eternal Head that arrived in Kostya's knowledge box when they were in Nur-Sultan. With a high degree of confidence, Kostya felt he could finally share the valuable information with his nomad comrades.

"Here is some information that could cost you your heads, guys. The Eternal Head is a group of actual people, living and ruling together," Kostya proclaimed. He sounded as if he expected genuine surprise.

"That is not a big deal," retorted Kenesary. "All parliaments and parties are groups of actual people despite all the evidence."

"No, I am not talking about NaroDAO. Everyone knows that NaroDAO is nothing but a forever-clapping Central Committee meeting that failed to end. As such, its members are still the same bunch of athletes, musicians, writers, hardworking farmers, and anyone else who got famous for anything but critical thinking. This group I am talking about has always been kept secret and they are behind everything that has been going on in the Soviet Union and Eurasia since Lenin's times."

"You mean it is a group of NKVD agents?" asked Kenesary, trying to see if he got it right.

"I wish you were right. That would warrant some diversity and possibility of interesting ideas. Unfortunately, the Eternal Head, my friends, is composed of a hundred clones of one and the same person," replied Kostya.

"Unbelievable! You mean there are other clones besides me and her?" asked Kenesary, slightly excited that it was not only about him and someone else anymore.

"Absolutely. And guess what? They have been around for a while! In the Soviet Union, and in some other countries. Why do you think they kept Lenin in the mausoleum all the time?" asked Kostya as if he were Sherlock Holmes.

"Oh, wow. To keep Lenin's genes intact. So they did not have to exhume the poor person and take his genes whenever necessary," said Kenesary, happy to show that he was no worse than Dr. Watson when it comes to figuring things out.

"Exactly. And for the exact same reason Lysenko must have prohibited genetics in the Soviet Union for so long. People were not supposed to understand genetic matters. Soviets tried really hard to cover up their discovery of cloning techniques, but their borders were more semi-permeable than they thought. Their first loss was Theodosius Dobzhansky, who was born in my native Ukraine. He managed to move to the United States thanks to the Rockefeller Foundation in 1927 and continued his work on *Drosophila melanogaster*, a fruit fly which helped discover the secrets of nature. Soviets were extremely angry that they lost this father of evolutionary biology. Nevertheless, their secret genetic research had to be done in secret laboratories throughout the Soviet Union, including in Kenesary's birthplace—Barsa-Kelmes."

"Are you telling me I may not be the first person to be cloned in Barsa-Kelmes?" inquired the last Kazakh khan.

"I am sorry, bro, but no, you are not. You think all these godless Soviet politicians, alpha males of the highest degree, did not want to multiply themselves in hundreds?"

"Well, there were other ways to do it. Right?"

"Not when you are under watchful eyes of the KGB..."

"It makes sense. Anyway, go on... You seem like you have a lot more to tell."

"Well, very few geneticists escaped the Soviet Union after Dobzhansky. The Soviets lost too many people during the revolutions, Stalin's purges, the World Wars, and mass famishes in Ukraine and Kazakhstan. They needed to secretly clone more geniuses in order to achieve their Cosmos exploration objectives. More importantly, they needed to apply cloning techniques to improve agricultural outcomes of five-year plans. So, they could not keep their methods completely secret. As a result, when the Soviet Union collapsed, one of the graduates of Timiryazev Agricultural Institute, a Uyghur..." Here Kostya winks at Amursana. "Born in Almaty, Kazakhstan, moves to the United States and starts working with monkeys and figures out how to clone people. *Nature Magazine* calls him 'chief of cloning'! And guess what? He was a good friend of Ansar Tolengitovich, your father. Or whatever you call a man who comes up with an idea and clones someone to produce you."

"Completely amazing! So, where are all these Lenins now?" asked Kenesary.

"Some of them have already passed away... Each time one of them dies, they make some kind of news about Lenin's monument falling down in some obscure location. It is a secret way of communication through the news. I think they are dispersed in different locations throughout Russia—anywhere from Sakhalin to Kaliningrad. Soviets came up with decentralization long before Satoshi Nakamoto."

"In that case, we have a serious adversary to face, my friends," said Amursana. He felt sad there were no other avatars and reincarnations he could meet. He felt he envied Kenesary a little bit here.

"Yes, we are lucky we only have Qozganov to face in Kazakhstan," said Kenesary.

"You never know," replied Kostya, and smiled with that mysterious Cossack smile of his.

He had to think about these new ideas. Was there any chance that nomads could actually survive such a totalitarian power? Was it worth putting the young people's lives at risk? Poor Amursana was already insane and young Kenesary could have a happy life somewhere in the West. Perhaps, the Pussy Riot was not worth all this.

* * *

When the trio, Tomyris, and Mels visited the Eye, Nur-Sultan's architectural masterpiece and library, the archeologist/librarian decided to test his friends. Having read a lot about Kenesary, participating in the shameful exhumation, and never figuring out what actually happened to the head, Mels was curious whether Amursana could meditate back to 1848, the year of the khan's tragic death.

"I heard you are quite a magician, my Uyghur Jungar. Could you please go back to the last khan's year of death and trace the fate of his head? I wonder what befell it."

"After seeing all these energetic fellow nomads and this all-seeing Eye, I feel I can do anything. Should I get in touch with any particular person who would know the fate of the head for sure?"

"Sure, get in touch with that Governor of Western Siberia, who supposedly received the khan's head from the Kyrgyz tribal leader. He would know, I think."

The reincarnation could not refuse his nephew's godfather. He sat cross-legged facing Ak Orda, the local White House, and went into silence. It took about ten minutes of awkward waiting before Amursana could connect to that tumultuous year.

Jesus Christ! These guys are killing each other again. What am I supposed to do with this head? Who do they think I am to enjoy this sight and reward them for such mischief? If Zilqara and other heads of the Middle Horde learn about this, all my friends' and relatives' businesses with Kazakhs will suffer losses. I should call the local imam and secretly bury this head.

I certainly don't want to face the local Muslim nomads' anger. We have put enough of them on fire for converting back to Islam and refusing to accept our religion. It took us decades to rectify our relationship with the Buddhist nomads for letting the Manchu delegates exhume Amursana to prove he was indeed dead. Twice. God bless the Empress's soul for finding wisdom not to give his body away to hang in Peking. It was enough to anger our very own Old Believer Cossacks with hanging Pugachev so ruthlessly.

We live in the nineteenth century. Revolutions are spreading all over Europe. I am not bringing that revolt to my dear Siberia. No way. Poor Kenesary. He should have accepted my advice and stopped fighting against people equipped so heavily. He would enjoy his life pretending to be an independent ruler.

May his soul rest in peace. No money shall I give for his head. Instead, I will go to Crimea and take a proper vacation from this whole affair. And I should see to it that a letter of condolence is sent to the Kazakh leaders. Sad but good.

Kenesary the Clone, having heard this, became convinced that the Soviets indeed invented the myth of the head to exercise symbolic power over the Kazakhs. They must have indeed read the Versailles Agreement in full. "It is a great power to be able to write a nation's history," he said to Mels.

"It is a great power to be conscious of that fact," replied Mels, in a professorial tone, touching his thick beard, which made him think of his academically-inclined father. "You are better off out of this country, without crypto though you may be."

"If there is no head in St. Petersburg, as Russian presidents used to say in the past, why do we keep asking for it?" inquired Tomyris, in a somewhat alarmed tone. She had become shrewd in Almaty business circles.

"Perhaps, Kazakhs want to think Russia owes them something," interjected Kostya, who found this Asian lady very interesting.

"Something that can never be returned," said Kenesary, but he sounded unconvinced. "Why would you want something like that?"

CHAPTER 18

THE SILICON VALLEY

———

2038, Nur-Sultan, Kazakhstan

When it became clear what kind of forces were at play, Kenesary got quite upset. Realizing that Mels had lost his Dogecoins and that Lenin was still ruling in the natural nomadic places, Kenesary had reason to be scared. Surrounded by strange friends and no real relatives, he needed to figure out what to do with his life. He was hoping to use his pedigree to make some money and career like his British schoolmates, but it turned out that his DNA could make him a political target instead. The founding father of the Soviet Union tolerated no royal blood, red though it may be.

With no inheritance but genes, Kenesary concluded that he would need an alternative strategy to emancipate himself and achieve financial liberty. This meant he would need to get a good education, no way around it, and preferably in the United States. Nadezhda Ivanovna would help with completing his schooling in England, but she would not spend a single cent on American education. Not on Kenesary in any case and not when Tomyris was no longer a curiosity from Barsa-Kelmes.

He still wanted to get a traditional Western education by completing his undergraduate degree. With a true nomadic queen's name, his mom Tomyris would not settle for anything less than Harvard for her young khan. She was obsessed with the idea of sending her son to "Garvard," as she pronounced it. Yet, she did not have that much money and Kenesary would have to study harder to get admitted to such a famous university. Now that he only had a few papers to submit to graduate from Attila, he had little chance to significantly improve his grades.

Even with Ivy League college degrees, both commoners and nobility had limited options and their lives were laid out in many ways. There were no shortcuts. Some were expected to continue their educational journeys at top law schools, medical programs, or business schools. Some donated their time and credentials to top consulting firms, investment banks, and neo-feudal technology companies. The best talent of the world, however, dreamed of becoming apprentices of the Silicon Valley wizards. Those wizards included some of the most influential people in both the Universe and the Metaverse. The wizards had one strict requirement—drop out as early as possible.

They wanted people to drop out of top universities, of course. They wanted those students to show commitment, to sell their souls for quick money. Much like Timm Thaler had to sell his laughter to get rich, college drop-outs were supposed to swap their intellectual joys for a quick fortune. It was supposed to be easier that way to pre-select next technology leaders, such as Bill and Mark, but it did not really matter. One simply had to go through this path in order to prove their dedication to the cause of the digital revolution.

That's why Kenesary strongly wanted to get into Harvard—only to drop out. It was very much like his life—carefully cloned to be a khan only to struggle to survive with a single mom. If he got into Harvard, he would instantly reject their offer and become a Peter fellow or maybe an intern at a64z. He had read Ben's book about Genghis Khan and realized that his true calling was to conquer the digital world. He did not want to spill the blood of commoners trying to repeat his ancestors' achievements.

The culture of ruthlessness and confrontation with anyone for the sake of confrontation had already proved to be devastating for the people of Central Asia and Russia who were mostly affected by Genghis Khan's legacy. Perhaps, a smarter way would be to renounce all this à la Buddha and meditate in luxurious houses of Northern California. He really did not want to waste his time and health by being involved in politics with no money or by mining uranium to fuel nuclear reactors operated by the people of the Eternal Head in Central Asia and Siberia.

"Kostya, do you realize that being a nomad is not actually about horses and steppes? You are here with us trying to revive nomadic civilization, but don't you think we are heading the wrong direction?" asked Kenesary.

"You are young, but you are right. In your great historian Dulati's history book from the sixteenth century there is a very clear explanation given by Kassym Khan, your ancestor. He said being a nomad is about being free politically. Do you know what political freedom means?"

"Polis is Greek for city. So, you mean freedom from the city?"

"Exactly. Look at what Americans did once they got rich. They began a massive urban flight. Free people avoid city life."

"Why are Kazakhs all moving to live in tiny apartments in huge cities then? Look at these skyscrapers the nomads have built!"

"Perhaps, they are not nomads anymore. They may have horses and a beautiful steppe, but they know very little about freedom."

"So what needs to be done?"

"People need to be serious about education, build global businesses, give back to their communities, think long term, and stick to their nomadic values."

"Easier said than done."

"The nomads usually think that easier done than said," smiled Kostya.

"I will try to be a nomad in the United States," said Kenesary.

"Take your chance," replied Kostya, almost sarcastically.

* * *

While thinking about his options, Kenesary realized he did not want to be a nomad rebel in this highly dangerous political environment. He could deal with Qozganov, of course, but if hundreds of Lenins were involved, it would be much better to emigrate. It was very obvious that no one cared much about the return of Kenesary in Kazakhstan. And no one cared about the reincarnation of his "uncle." Poor Amursana… he was indeed badly affected by all his experiences. His mental health had gotten better in Kazakhstan, but he still was convinced that he was a reincarnation.

Kenesary believed Amursana could feel he was a normal Uyghur man if only he were allowed to talk to his relatives again. That was not possible for one more generation. His people were happily passing internships, and they saw him as a traitor of Uyghurs, Islam, and China. This was despite the fact that Amursana spoke Uyghur when he meditated, refrained from eating pork, and watched every Chinese movie shot in Xinjiang.

Genuine cultural transformation of a nation was supposed to take at least forty years. Even the Soviets could not entirely manage to transform their subjects in seventy years. That's why the Eternal Head became more aggressive in the second decade of the millennium and requested a forty-year extension by imposing economic sanctions and vaccine bans on themselves. They found the Iron Curtains so much more efficient and badly wanted them back.

Kostya and his AI Pugachev proved to be very interesting. They were obsessed with their nomad ideas, and Kenesary felt he had done enough by being born for them. At the very least, he got a great experience for his college application by participating in the organization of the World Nomad Games and assisting a Uyghur refugee with mental health issues.

He really learned a lot from Amursana in addition to helping him out and taking him all the way to the queen and to Kazakhstan. There was no point of mentioning in his university application that Kenesary was a clone of the last khan of the Kazakhs. It could only hurt his chances. Although he would definitely mention that he met the queen of the United Kingdom. His dream college had already been under much criticism for being overly elitist. As a Central Asian man and a son of a widow from Kazakhstan, he figured, he had much more chance of getting in. It was time to leave Nur-Sultan, take Amursana back to England, fly to Massachusetts to visit a university campus, and then go to the Silicon Valley.

Kostya accepted Kenesary's decision with sadness, but he was not as sad as the khan expected. Perhaps, AI Pugachev foresaw such an outcome. Who knew. Nevertheless, Kostya promised he would write a letter of recommendation for Kenesary with the help of AI Pugachev. The offer sounded genuine and promising. With all that AI Pugachev could do, Kenesary wondered if the kings of the Silicon Valley would notice him too. Kostya smiled with that great Cossack smile of his. "We will look into the matter," he replied. "Meanwhile, AI Pugachev got you some Air Astana business flight tickets to the UK, ten-year visa to America, and an economy flight ticket from London to Boston. Isn't that what you Kazakhs and Uyghurs love so much?" Kenesary felt excited, whereas Amursana decided to withhold his objection.

As they were leaving Nur-Sultan, discussing their time spent in the steppe and looking forward to getting to the West, two men grabbed their seats close to the nomad rebels and began carefully recording them on their dark eyeglass-installed cameras. One was Ivan Andreyevich, dressed in a black robe and assigned to work as a priest at the Orthodox church in Fort Ross, California, and the other one was Eldar Jose, dressed in fashionable clothes and recently assigned the new ambassador of the Republic of Kazakhstan to the United States of America. They had to watch Kenesary grow a little bit more and make sure that Qozganov would deliver on his promise by 2040, as was suggested by The Shaman. The true and only head of the last khan belonged to the people. No other head would pass a genetic test.

EPILOGUE

1750, Burabay, Middle Horde, Qazaq Khanate
The forty days following the White Camel sacrifice brought
contentment back to the khan's yurt. Topysh the Beautiful
mastered some new asanas, and Abylai Khan memorized
some new verses from the Quran. Both were at peace. On
the forty-first day, however, the Khan woke up much earlier
for his morning prayer.

"What happened, my Soul?" asked Topysh.

"I saw another strange dream..."

"Do you want me to interpret it or would you rather wait
for Master Bukhar Zhyrau's return?"

"I will wait for him," replied the Khan.

Seven days later, Master Bukhar Zhyrau returned from
Bayanaul. His unusual, saintly voice could be heard from
afar in the silent steppe. After spending a day and a night
full of music, meals, and conversation, he was ready to listen
to the Khan the next day. Abylai Khan retold his dream in
the following manner.

"An almost invisible headless dragon roamed among the
hills and forests of the steppe. The dragon walked backward,

headed by its tail, which was unusually long and fat. I could not bear that... And the hills were as high as Mount Okjetpes, except instead of the stones that make up the Mount, I could see yurts...thousands of them, one above and next and below the other. Yurts over yurts over yurts, with people living inside like some bees, which give Bashkirs the best of their honey. It looked so real to me that I started reading ayat-al-kursi and woke up, all thanks be to Allah. I can still vividly see all this, and I have no idea what to make of it, Komekei..."

Bukhar Zhyrau was listening to Abylai with closed eyes, as if trying to share in the dream. Then he said: "This reminds me of Asan Qaigy's saying, if you recall. He forecasted that there would come a time when a pickerel would behead a pine. I am afraid such times are inevitable and your dream only confirms it. Let's hope that our descendants will stick to our ways of life, traditions, and religion. Perhaps, they will survive and what you have seen shall pass. As for now, put your trust in God and let's solve the challenges of today. Stop dreaming and wake up, Qazaq."

ACKNOWLEDGMENTS

———

Barsa-Kelmes has taken me around one year to write. I owe it to Professor Eric Koester at the Creator Institute for accepting me into his creative writing program for first-time authors. It was fascinating to work with my editors, David Grandouiller and Alan Zatkow. The way David and Alan treated this book's characters with curiosity, respect, and empathy helped me understand my story better. Thank you for bearing with my procrastination and erratic schedule.

I became interested in Eurasian history while studying at Duke University, where inspiring professors, such as Bruce Lawrence, Ebrahim Moosa, Göknar Erdağ, and Elena Maksimova had powerful influence on developing my understanding of other cultures and people. I also thank my professors at Eurasian National University and my classmates at Oxford University for their constant encouragement and stimulating conversations.

Special thanks the people who preordered my book and made its publication possible. You rock:

Aralbek Berikuly
Asset Altybayev
Svetlana Mendigaliyeva
Aslan Nazaraliyev
Almas Tuyakbayev
Aigerim Kaliyeva
Olzhas Zholdassov
Zubair Chao
Thomas Rogstad
Trey Sherard
Rustam Shokamanov
Sanat Batpen
Becky Hoai
Daria Fedorova
Igor Ganichev
Aiko Kokkozova
Salta Zhangaliyeva
Galym Imanbayev
Malika Aubakirova
Anuar Unaibekov
Daniyar Timerbulatov
Damir Okashev
Nurmukhammed Dossybayev
Almira Zakiyeva
Iskander Rakhman
Bauyrzhan Kikanov
David Levi
Adat Adilkhan
Kanat Kozhakhmet

Talgat Sailov
Arman Tokanov
Bayram Kenci
Adil Nurgozhin
Apysheva Leila
Mansur Wadalawala
Renat Bek
Zhanibek Datbayev
Bayan Kaliyeva
Elena Krylovetskaya
Alibi Sansyzbay
Yerden Kussain
Siyeona Chang
Kateryna Lukash
Anuar Unaibekov
Ellie Zhussuyeva
Nurasyl Shokeyev
Aigerim Ussenova
Togzhan Ibrayeva
Nader Mohyuddin
Altynay Tanasheva
Beksultanhozha Anuarov
Andrey Shovkoplyas
Nikolay Berezhnoy
Wade Kovash
Togzhan Sultan
Dilyara Issamadiyeva
Gulmira Baigabulova
Olzhas Bateyev
Adilbek Primbetov

Almaz Kungozhin
Nurislam Tursynbek
Arkalyk Akash
Tauyekel Bek
Timur Baimagambetov
Aigerim Sadbayeva
Assem Kunakbayeva
Samat Toibayev
Gaukhar
Kassymzhanova
Dinara Jarmukhanova

Baur Bektemirov
Baoli Zhao
Eric Koester
Steve McIntosh
Arin Meirembayev
Bryan Miller
Yerlan Uteulin
Brenden De Matos-Ala
Shawn Ruggeiro
Tlek Zeinullayev
Elvira de Jong